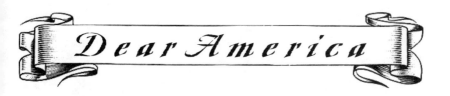

Where Have All the Flowers Gone?

The Diary of
Molly MacKenzie Flaherty

BY ELLEN EMERSON WHITE

Scholastic Inc. New York

This diary is based upon actual historical events, but *all* names and many locations have been changed. For example, there *is* a Veterans' Administration Hospital located in the general area of Boston that has been described, but the one in the diary is entirely fictionalized, in order to protect the privacy of people who actually served in Vietnam — and worked at VA hospitals, in Boston and elsewhere. This same strategy was used throughout the book, in an attempt to walk the line between accuracy and fiction. Any similarities to the identities or experiences of actual people — other than well-known public figures, such as President Lyndon Johnson and Dr. Martin Luther King — are an absolute and complete coincidence.

Boston, Massachusetts
1967

December 25, 1967
Brighton, Massachusetts

I really like Jason. I wonder if he likes me, too.

And I can't believe I just wrote that. A brand-new diary, and *that's* how I start off? I'm using a pen, too, so I can't cross it out. That is, I could, but it would look terrible to have a big mistake right on the first page. Although if my brother was here, it might be the perfect way to keep him from reading this behind my back, which I'm pretty sure he's been doing with all my diaries and journals for years. If I kept writing long pages about Jason, and how cute he is, and how much I wish he would ask me out, and on, and on — Patrick might get so bored that he'd never bother picking up one of my diaries again. That might actually make it worth doing. Then again, if I *really* wanted to frighten him, I could waste a few pages mooning over Paul McCartney, and how dreamy I think he is. And how perfect we are for each other — except that Patrick would never buy that, since he knows that when it comes to musicians, that guy from the Doors, Jim Morrison, is the one I think is incredibly handsome. Probably not perfect for me, because he seems pretty wacky, but *handsome?* Wow.

But, Patrick isn't here, and that's probably what I should be writing about right now. We're all pretending that it's a normal Christmas, and we feel like celebrating — but it isn't, and we don't. Still, we're putting on a pretty good show, because of my niece and nephew. Actually, Gregory isn't even a year old, so I don't think he would know the difference one way or the other, but Jane is three and Christmas is a big deal for her. That's why everyone has been laughing, and joking, and *having a whole lot of fun* all day long.

Pretending that my brother isn't in Vietnam.

I don't want to think about it, but I can't seem to think about much of anything else. It doesn't help that practically every time we turn on the television, there's some news report about Vietnam, and mainly what you see is really young, tired-looking soldiers carrying some wounded guy on a stretcher over to a helicopter. Or Walter Cronkite or some other newscaster is talking about the "body count." Body count doesn't sound that awful, until you realize that it means how many

Americans — and Vietnamese people — were *killed* this week.

The first time I heard the term "friendly fire" on the news, I had to ask my father what it meant. He didn't seem to want to answer, but finally he said that it's when American soldiers get wounded or killed — by other Americans, by mistake. Gee, Dad, that sounds *really* friendly, I said, and he just mumbled and shrugged and went back to the sports pages.

When people find out my brother is over there, they assume he was drafted, and that the whole situation is very tragic — but no, it's worse than that. Patrick *volunteered*.

His eighteenth birthday was on June 28th, and right after we had breakfast that morning, Patrick went straight downtown to join the Marines. He'd been planning it for weeks, since my parents had refused to sign the paperwork to let him join while he was still seventeen. So we were all expecting it, but it was still sort of a shock to have him finish off his bacon and eggs (plus half of mine, of course), and then hustle out to Commonwealth Avenue to catch the subway.

My father was mad, because Patrick had three college football scholarship offers he was throwing away, but it was pretty easy to see that he was also proud. He fought all over Europe in the Army in World War II, and almost all of my uncles and cousins have served, too. My mother was just upset. She's a very quiet person — especially compared to my father, and whenever the subject of the war comes up, she disappears into the kitchen, or starts doing laundry, or goes into their bedroom and closes the door.

I remember calling my sister, Brenda, that morning to see what she thought, and she just sighed and said that Patrick was going to do what he was going to do and that she wanted to stay out of it. Which was pretty much what I expected her to say — she's a lot like my mother that way — but I figured it couldn't hurt to ask.

And what did I think? What *do* I think? Well, Patrick came home that afternoon, gave me his usual grin, and said, "So?"

"You're a big jerk," I said.

He grinned again. "Yup. A big *patriotic* jerk."

"And a moron and a cretin and an idiot and a dolt," I said. "But — Happy Birthday, anyway."

We both thought that was pretty funny — although we may not be the best authorities, since we think *most* things are pretty funny. Brenda can be pretty sarcastic, but as a rule, she's a lot more serious than we are, so it's really easy to make her mad. My parents, too. But Patrick always says that that just means we should be twice as obnoxious.

That is, unless I say it first.

No matter how hard I try, though, I can't make anything about Vietnam, and the war, seem funny.

I bet Patrick can't, either.

Later —

The house is so quiet. Since Dad had last night and today off, he had to go down to the firehouse tonight. My brother-in-law is working the same tour, so Brenda took Jane and Gregory home to put them to bed. All of my other relatives went home, too, except for my grandmother, who's spending the night. She was tired, though, so she went to sleep early.

I helped my mother clean up for a while, and then I took our dog, Maggie, for a walk. I say our dog, but I guess she's really my dog. I was riding the subway aboveground up Commonwealth Avenue, when I saw a black puppy running in and out of traffic. So, I jumped off at the next stop and tried to catch her. She was really skinny, and scared, but I finally got her to come over to me by Packard's Corner. Then, I picked her up and carried her the rest of the way home. I could feel her shaking the whole time, but every so often, her tail would wag nervously, and I already knew that I had to keep her.

I wasn't sure if it was a good idea to bring her in, since we still had our shepherd, Fred, then. He was very old and frail, and I thought a puppy might upset him. I *knew* it would upset my parents, but I was more worried about Fred. But having her around perked Fred up, and my parents didn't really mind, since Maggie was so sweet. She's over fifty pounds now, and looks like a black Irish setter. She's not the sort of dog who's good at learning tricks — other than fetching, which she'll do all day. Mainly, she just likes to follow you around, cuddle up next to you, and rest her head on you as much as possible.

And you know what? That's fine with me. She loves everyone in the family, but I'm glad that she almost always sleeps on my bed, because otherwise, I think my feelings might be hurt.

I also found all three of our cats and — well, my

father always says that it's really not safe to let me leave the house by myself. Last year, I ran into a big, stray collie mix, but luckily, Fitzy — who's assigned to Dad's engine company — agreed to adopt her. I just can't walk away when I see an animal in trouble, but so far, I've been pretty good at finding homes for them quickly. Except for our newest cat, Joyce, who's so mean that no one else would take her. She likes my mother, though, and she tolerates me, so it all worked out. My father makes a big point of only patting her when he's wearing oven mitts, but I think he's just being silly. Patrick will tiptoe over to pat Joyce when he's all suited up in his football gear, or wearing hockey pads or something, but — well, he's pretty goofy, too.

Boy, I really miss him. This will sound stupid, but it doesn't even feel like our house when he isn't here.

After I walked Maggie tonight — and threw a few snowballs for her to fetch, I went into the living room to see what was on television. I *love* television. The big family present under the tree today was a brand-new color set, which is really neat. We've always had black-and-white televisions, so being able to watch in color is going to be cool. Or, as my cousin Nina put it, "far out." I sometimes say stuff like "far out" and "groovy" around my friends, but it sounds kind of dumb if you use them in regular conversations. To me, anyway.

It turned out that there was a documentary about Vietnam on tonight, and I decided I could get away with watching at least part of it before my mother came in. I sat on the couch with Maggie sprawled out next to me. Our cat Eric jumped up and looked furious to see Maggie taking "his spot," but then he curled up by my other leg and went to sleep.

The documentary had been filmed in a town in Virginia, and the reporter interviewed a bunch of different people to get their opinions about the war. It was pretty much what you'd expect — the students were against it, the stodgy businessmen were for it, but then, just as my mother came into the room, they started interviewing a guy whose brother had died in Vietnam. They were going to ask his mother questions, too. I jumped up and flicked the channel over to *Family Affair*. I think my mother had heard at least part of the interview, but she just put a plate of homemade cookies down on the coffee table and sat in the rocking chair she likes.

We watched Buffy and Jody and Mr. French for a few minutes. In color! Which made the show seem — well, even more stupid than it usually is, actually.

"Why do you always want to watch those things?" my mother asked.

That sounded like the beginning of a not-very-fun conversation. "Because I think Cissy is completely mod, and I want to be just like her," I said.

My mother just looked at me.

Well, okay, I can't stand Cissy. Better she should be named "Prissy." Maybe I should have said I had a big crush on Uncle Bill, instead.

And my mother was still looking at me.

Okay. Why did I watch — and read — everything about Vietnam I could find? I've been doing it since way before Patrick even joined the Marines, so it isn't just that. But it seems like so many people have such strong feelings about the war — one way or the other — and when you listen to them talk (or yell, mostly), I feel like I'm agreeing with parts of *both* sides, and that can't be right.

"Because if I keep watching, maybe it'll start making sense," I said finally.

My mother sighed, looking very serious — and sad. "I don't think it ever will, Molly."

No, probably not. But I figure it can't hurt to try.

Later —

I don't know why I keep writing and writing like this, but my father made a big point of giving this diary to me this morning. He'd even wrapped it himself. That surprised me, since my mother is the one who almost always picks out everyone's presents.

"Maybe he figures if you stay busy writing things down, you won't talk quite as much," Brenda said, when I showed it to her later.

Well — it's a theory.

Anyway, it's a very nice diary. Cloth-covered, with little daisies, and blank pages instead of dates already marked inside. I got my first diary when I was about eight years old, and each one I've had ever since follows pretty much the same pattern. For the first few weeks, I write every day, even if it's boring stuff like "I got up. I brushed my teeth. I went to school. I came home." Then, by February, it might be every two or three days. And by May? Well, lots and lots of empty pages, for the most part. But unmarked pages takes the pressure off — I can just write whenever I feel like I have something to say. I guess the best thing about writing in a diary is that you can share your feelings, complain as much as you want, worry, fret, obsess, sulk — and no one else ever has to know about it.

I can't picture Patrick writing in the diary Dad gave him right before he shipped out, since he's always hated doing his English assignments. Patrick's really smart, but he's just never had the patience to sit around doing homework, when he could be outside throwing a ball or hitting a hockey puck or something. He barely studied at all, but he still managed to get B's and only a few C's, without putting in any effort. Brenda never studied, either, but she would get B's, and a few A's here and there. I study *a lot*, but that's only because I need all A's to get into a really good college, and then apply to veterinary school after I graduate. I keep hearing that it's easier to get into medical school than it is a veterinary program. My goal is to go to Cornell's veterinary school, because they're supposed to be the best.

My Uncle Jim — who means well — once told me, very kindly, that if I wanted, I could always get a job working in a pet store someday. I usually don't mind starting trouble — okay, I *enjoy* it — but, in that particular case, it seemed easier just to nod and agree with him. But I have a feeling that if my name was *Mark*, instead of Molly, that thought never would have crossed his mind.

I don't know. I hope I'm wrong about that.

After *Family Affair*, my mother and I watched *The Carol Burnett Show*, because Ella Fitzgerald was the main guest star tonight. My father says that once you've heard Frank Sinatra, you never need to listen to another singer for the rest of your life — but I'd put Ella up in that category, too. She's the best.

I could tell my mother was tired, but she's not just worried about Patrick tonight — she's worried about Dad. And Hank, my brother-in-law, too. There are always so many fires during the holidays, mostly because people forget to water their Christmas trees and leave the lights on, or — even worse — decorate them with *lighted candles*. Since I've grown up hearing about fire safety for as long as I can remember, the thought of that just makes me shiver.

Dad's a captain down in the South End, and his house is one of the busiest — if not *the* busiest — in the city. I like to go down there and visit him, although it makes my mother nervous, because it's a pretty bad neighborhood. Dad describes it as being "lively." *Big* understatement. His engine company, and the truckies, fight fires, but they end up having to help a lot of crime and accident victims, too, especially at night. And things have been a lot more tense down there since the bad riots in Roxbury and Dorchester last summer. Along with the looting and protesting and everything, people were doing stuff like throwing rocks at the firefighters who were trying to put out fires in their neighborhoods. It was terrible.

Firefighters in Boston are called "jakes." The stars in the department — and every company has a couple — are called "good jakes." There have been a lot of problems in the department recently, because a couple of jakes have died from carbon monoxide poisoning during routine fires. Dad thinks the Chief is going to take their air masks out of service soon, which means there will be lots of cases of smoke inhalation. And some of the members' coats have been catching on fire unexpectedly — but nobody knows why. So, it's scary. When Dad comes home late from his tour, it almost always means that he was at the emergency room, getting some oxygen or having small burns treated — but we never really talk about it. You just *don't*, when you're related to someone who's on the line.

Instead, you worry a lot. Sure, my parents fight sometimes, but they always try to make up before Dad goes to work. And if he yells at one of us, he makes sure to apologize before he leaves. Last spring, I got really mad at him about something dumb, and wouldn't come out of my room to say good-bye. Then, I felt awful, and I took the subway downtown — without permission — and walked over to Tremont Street, so that I could just say, "Hi, Dad," really fast, and then go right back home. I think we both felt a whole lot better, afterwards.

My father's father was a firefighter for thirty years. (He was only fifty-nine when he died of emphysema, probably from all of those years of inhaling massive amounts of smoke.) My Uncle Jim and my Uncle Colin are jakes, too, along with my cousin Kyle and, of course, my brother-in-law, Hank. Knowing Patrick, when he gets out of the service (I'm never, ever going to say *if*, no matter what), he'll probably join the department, too. My cousin Ray, who likes to brag that he's different, is a police officer.

It all adds up to a lot of worried days and sleepless nights for everyone else in the family.

Like tonight.

December 26, 1967

When Dad got home this morning, he was tired, but he barely smelled of smoke at all. That's always a good sign. When he opens the door and the whole house suddenly fills with that familiar wet, smoky smell, we all know he had a tough tour. He said last night was mostly just nuisance fires — garbage bins, a couple of cars, things like that. There was one fire at a bar, which could have been bad, but it was just down the street from the firehouse, so they were able to put it out right away. And — most important — no one got hurt. Whenever Dad gets home after a tour when no one even had minor injuries, he always walks in smiling.

So, it was a nice day, although we were all disappointed when the mail came and there were no letters from my brother. We've only gotten one letter from him so far, and it didn't say very much. Just that he was in a place called Danang (I had to look it up on a map that I saved from an issue of *National Geographic*), it was unbelievably hot, and he was waiting to get his orders and find out where he would be going next. He also said that we shouldn't worry about him, and underlined it three times.

All of which means we don't even have an address where we can write to him yet. It seems like forever, but he's only been over there for about two weeks, and I guess the mail is pretty slow. We've already written him some letters, anyway, and we'll just wait and address the envelopes as soon as we find out where to send them.

Marines have to serve thirteen months in Vietnam. The Army only has to serve a year — I'm not sure why. So that means that we won't see him again until *next* January, unless — well, I'm just praying that there isn't an "unless."

Unless the war ends. That would be a good "unless."

A wonderful "unless."

But I don't think it will happen anytime soon.

I hope I'm wrong.

December 27, 1967

We got two letters from Patrick today! Mom was so relieved she almost started crying. Our mailman, Mr. Owens, knew we were waiting for anything from Vietnam, so he came right up and knocked on the door instead of just putting the mail in our box.

In the first letter, Patrick wrote that he was about to fly to a place called Dong Ha, and then he'd be going to join his unit somewhere up near the DMZ. The DMZ is the Demilitarized Zone, and I guess it's the border between North Vietnam and South Vietnam. I think it was originally set up as a neutral zone, to separate the two parts of the country — literally — and to help keep the peace. Most of our Marine troops are guarding and defending the DMZ from the Viet Cong guerillas (the VC) and the North Vietnamese Army (the NVA). I wish I understood more about what's happening over there. People always seem to be so busy arguing about the war — "It's evil and immoral!" or "My country, right or wrong!" — but I never really hear anyone discussing the *details*. Just that we're fighting against Communism, and that the South Vietnamese people either can't — or won't — do it for themselves.

But, it has to be more complicated than that, right?

Patrick's letter about going to Dong Ha was pretty short, because he wanted to mail it before he left Danang. He said that all he'd been doing since he got to Vietnam (he calls it "in-country") was standing in lines, and that everything was a lot more disorganized than he had expected. Other than that, he mainly just talked about how hot it was, and how there was this constant, awful smell in the air, so he was mostly breathing through his mouth.

The next letter was from Dong Ha, and he was finally able to send us his address. He's been assigned to Golf Company, in the 3rd Battalion, 26th Marines, and he'll be stationed at a place called Khe Sanh. I found Khe Sanh on my map, in the very top left corner of South Vietnam. It seems to be about as far as you can go, without actually being in North Vietnam, or Laos or Cambodia. In the letter, he said not to worry (except that the more times he writes that, the less I believe it), that Khe Sanh is considered a very quiet area. Out in what he described as "the boonies," pretty much in the middle of nowhere. If it really *is* that quiet, I hope he spends his whole tour there.

Mom and I sat down to address the little pile of our unmailed letters to him, and then I took them down to the post office for her. Patrick just wrote "Free" in the corner of his envelopes — which seems like the least the government can do for their soldiers.

"How's he doing over there?" Mr. Trabowsky asked, when I paid him for the postage.

I told him what *I* wanted to hear. "He's fine. They're sending him to Khe Sanh."

Mr. Trabowsky, who is a World War II veteran, frowned. "Isn't that where all those hill battles were last spring?"

Instantly, I was scared. What hill battles? I'll have to go to the library as soon as I can and look that up. I remember reading about a really big hill battle in November, but that was in a place called Dak To, which was much further south than Khe Sanh. That was probably the battle Mr. Trabowsky meant, and he just got the name wrong.

I hope.

My mother had given me a list of things to pick up on my way home, like milk, cat food, paper towels, candles, and a bunch of other stuff. I can't wait until I can drive — only about three months left until I can take the test! — but we're within walking distance of lots of stores and restaurants down on Harvard Avenue and over on Brighton Ave. I had to climb over a lot of snowdrifts, but, you know, that's why you wear *boots*.

I like my neighborhood. Allston is part of Brighton, which is part of Boston, but it doesn't really feel like a city. There are some brownstones, and tenements, and triple-decker buildings, but we have a house and a yard. It's a pretty small yard — not big enough for Maggie to be able to get any exercise — but there's a really nice park right up the street and I take her there to run every day.

Patrick used to let me tag along with him, so I grew up playing baseball and football up there, too. The only rule was that since I was one of the only girls, I wasn't allowed to cry if someone tackled me, or took me out at second base, trying to break up a double play. So I never did, even though it *really* hurt sometimes. Eddie Finnegan was probably the most competitive guy we knew — except for my brother — so, he used to slam into me all the time. But then he'd get really upset, and help me up, and apologize for about an hour. One time, when I was about ten, he made me so mad that I "accidentally" tackled him after the play was dead — and he actually broke his arm. I felt terrible, but he thought it was funny, once he got over being embarrassed.

Eddie's in Vietnam right now, too — one of the only other guys from our high school who's there. There are other older guys who have already gone and come back — some of them got home safely, and a few others weren't that lucky. I didn't know Carl Roarke, because he graduated in 1964, but he was a Marine and lost his leg over there. And it makes me sick to think about it, but two other boys from my school have been killed in the war. There's a plaque on the wall in the main hallway dedicated to each of them. The only one I knew, Peter Korbett, was a running back on the football team, and my brother played with him for two seasons.

Since Patrick left, my mother has been going to mass every single morning, and she says she always sees Mrs. Finnegan. If Dad's not working, he goes, too. Anyway, I hope Eddie's okay. I don't know much about what he's doing over there, except that he's in the Army, not the Marines. I've been wanting to write to him, but I feel shy about it. Mostly because he's older — and *really* cute, I guess. And when I look at that, it makes me sound really immature. I'll try to remember to ask Mom to get his address next time she sees his mother.

I'm not sure what I think about church, and God. Well, I'm not sure what I think about much of anything these days, so why should Catholicism be any different? But I do pray — mostly just to keep my family safe —

and some mornings, I go along with my mother to keep her company. We *always* go on Sundays and holidays — no arguments allowed. And we never, ever eat meat on Fridays. I don't like fish, so week after week, I end up having scrambled eggs or a grilled cheese sandwich for supper that night.

It's almost ten, and I think I'll stop so I can go watch *The Jonathan Winters Show*. In the paper today, it said that the Doors were going to be his musical guests.

Speaking of cute . . .

December 29, 1967

Mom and I put a care package together today to mail to Patrick. Candy, stationery, pens, a toothbrush, some soap, and other stuff he might need. I put in a Red Sox cap, too, although I'm not sure soldiers are allowed to wear things like that. But he can maybe keep it in his pack for good luck. Brenda brought over some chocolate brownies she made, and Dad's contribution was all of the football articles he's been cutting out of the newspapers every day.

After I took Maggie out, I came in here to my room to read and listen to music. That was the plan, anyway. I got some really nice books for Christmas, but I couldn't concentrate, so I decided to write for a little while.

Betsy Healy is having a New Year's Eve party, and my parents don't want me to go. She's a senior, but I know her pretty well, so I was invited. My best friend, Theresa, is supposed to be going, too. My father thinks I'm too young, but I am a junior — and I reminded him that it wasn't *my* idea to skip third grade. So it's not my fault that my friends are all a year or two older. In elementary school, my teachers wanted me to skip two grades, but my mother said one was enough. At the time, she told me that it might be hard for me to make friends if I was too much younger than everyone else. Once I was in junior high, I figured out that she'd also been trying to protect Patrick's feelings. If I'd skipped two grades, I would have been in his class. Patrick is smart, but no one was suggesting that he get promoted a grade ahead. He never seemed to mind, but whenever we had a fight when we were little, he'd always call me something like "smarty-pants." That one didn't bother me very much, so he went back to his old favorite of calling me a baby. *That* name would upset me every single time.

Now he calls me "kid," in this I'm-cooler-than-you-could-ever-*dream*-of-being way. I don't mind, but I complain a lot, so that he won't switch and come up with some nickname I really hate. Like, it would drive me crazy if he called me — except, wait a minute. In case he reads this behind my back sometime, I don't think I'll give him any ideas.

Better safe than sorry.

December 30, 1967

I finally managed to convince my parents to let me go to the party, since Betsy's house is only a few blocks away. She's right down on Quint Avenue, so I can walk there in less than five minutes. I feel a little guilty, though, because I didn't tell them that her parents aren't going to be home. They didn't ask — I guess they just assumed they would be — so, technically, I didn't lie. But it feels like a lie.

Well, maybe it's just a *fib*.

Theresa and I spent about an hour on the phone tonight, trying to decide what we should wear to the party. People who don't know Theresa very well think she's completely confident and sure of herself, because she's really opinionated and involved in a million different things as school — but, like me, she's actually pretty shy. We're just good at faking it. Our other good friend, Laurel, was going to come, too, but now she has to stay home, because her parents are having a big party for all of their relatives. I asked Betsy what people were going to be wearing, and she just said, "Oh, *you* know." "Oh, yeah, absolutely," I said. "I was just checking."

So much for that strategy.

I guess I'll use my father as a judge. If he doesn't like my outfit — whatever it is — then it will probably be just right.

It really upsets him when I wear jeans, because he doesn't think "it's proper for a young lady." But they're so comfortable, that I love them. They look funky, too. Especially bell-bottoms. I'd wear them every day, if I could. At school, we're *required* to wear skirts or dresses, but I always change right into capri pants or jeans as soon as I get home.

I wonder if Jason is going to the party. In case he

does, I should maybe wear something nice. For the record, yes, I really *do* like him. I think. No, I do. Definitely. Yeah. He probably won't notice what I have on one way or the other, but if I start writing, "Why doesn't he like me? What's wrong with me?" stuff, I'm going to get on my *own* nerves.

Enough writing. I think I'll go back to reading.

January 1, 1968

Well, Happy New Year. I guess.

I was really looking forward to Betsy's party, but I ended up not having very much fun. At all. It was mostly seniors, plus a bunch of people who already graduated. Most of them are in college, but some of them are working regular jobs, instead. Because of the draft, a lot more people from Brighton go to college these days.

Jason was there, but Cathy Watkins was hanging all over him the whole night. They're not even going out, but she kept touching his hair and fixing his collar and stuff like that, as if they were.

And — he definitely didn't seem to mind.

I'm not even sure why I like him so much, but I guess I've had a crush on him practically going back to when we used to sit next to each other in fourth grade. He has black curly hair and brown eyes, and he's really tall. He wears glasses, but they look good on him, I think. He also gets good grades — at least, in science and math — and he's on the track team. When we were in elementary school, we always used to talk about the Red Sox, but now, he doesn't seem to like girls who know about sports. So — okay, I admit it — when I'm around him, I guess I kind of pretend I don't. Theresa gives me grief about that, and — she has a point.

Patrick thinks Jason's a punk, but I'm pretty sure he wouldn't be happy unless I started dating someone on the football team. Because they're friends of his, most of the guys on the team are really nice to me, but a lot of them have spent so much time around our house or scrimmaging up in Ringer Playground, that they feel more like extra brothers than anything else.

Plus, the truth is that I don't look right, anyway. They all date cheerleaders, and girls who are — I don't know — *graceful*. I'm pretty clumsy, especially if I try to wear heels. For school and church, I mostly stick to loafers and flats. And my hair is — nothing special.

Sometimes I wear a ponytail, but usually, I just part it in the middle.

Seeing Jason hanging around Cathy was depressing, but that wasn't why I had such a bad time. At least, it wasn't the only reason. Theresa and I felt stupid because almost everyone else was drinking beer — *a lot* of beer, and I think there were even some people upstairs smoking marijuana. Pot. Weed. Grass. You're supposed to say "grass," if you're cool.

But I'm probably not cool, because I'm curious about what it would be like to smoke pot, but not curious enough to find out. You always hear such terrible things about drugs, so I think it's too dangerous. I mean, there are all those stories about people who take LSD and are never normal again.

"This isn't much fun," Theresa said, as we stood in a corner of the jam-packed living room, each holding a bottle of Coke and barely able to hear over the sound of a Beach Boys record playing at top volume.

No, it sure wasn't. People were getting loud, and Betsy Healy was a little drunk, but also looking upset because some of the basketball players were doing stuff like throwing couch pillows around and knocking things over. Her parents were going to be really mad, if they found out about all of this.

"Maybe we should just go," Theresa said.

It was definitely an idea. Instead, we went into the kitchen, where it was a little more quiet. It was easy to tell the college students apart from the high school kids, because almost all of them had much longer hair and they weren't acting as rowdy. I recognized a bunch of people who had graduated with Patrick, who must have been on Christmas break from college, including Audrey Taylor. Patrick has always had a thing for her, but he never asked her out because — well, I'm not sure why. I think he was too worried about being cool, sometimes. Lots of girls had crushes on him, but he usually only went out with cheerleaders. Brenda and I always yelled at him about that — especially because there were swell people like Audrey around. She ended up going out with their class valedictorian, Keith Erksted. And it looked like she was here with him tonight, which wouldn't make Patrick too happy.

When she saw me, she smiled. "Hi, Molly. Having a good time?"

"Yeah," I said. "It's nifty."

She laughed. "That's one word for it."

"Couldn't be niftier," Theresa said, and went over to talk to Edith Ames, who was home on vacation from the University of Vermont.

"I heard Patrick left," Audrey said.

"Yeah, a few weeks ago," I said. "He's up near the DMZ."

Audrey looked worried. "Do you think he's okay?"

"I don't know," I said. What else *could* I say? "I hope so." I motioned towards Keith, who was talking to a group of guys over by the back door. "You two are still going out?"

"No," Audrey said quickly. "I just came with him because — well, I hadn't seen him since school started, and he called, and —" She blinked a few times. "Well. You know."

I grinned, because I couldn't help thinking that Patrick had been doubly stupid never to ask her out. Although I probably won't mention it in my next letter to him, because it might make him sad. Then I turned, because I thought I heard Keith and those other guys talking about Vietnam — and my brother.

"Yeah, well, Flaherty just must have played too many games without wearing his helmet," one of them was saying, and the rest of them all laughed.

"Hey! Are you talking about Patrick?" I asked, making sure that my voice carried across the room.

A couple of the guys looked embarrassed, but the rest just stared right back at me.

"Yeah," Jeff Yancey — who had a beard now, and was wearing a peace necklace — said. "You have a problem with that?"

Big problem. So, I nodded.

"He's a baby-killer," Jeff said. "Don't you have a problem with *that*?"

Theresa had come over to stand next to me. "Let's just go," she muttered. "He's not going to listen to you, so it isn't worth it."

Defending my brother was definitely worth it. And no Flaherty *ever* backed down, anyway; we weren't raised that way. "He's serving his country," I said. "And none of you have the right to criticize him while you're hiding in college just to stay out of the draft." Okay, some of them, like Keith, would have been in college, anyway — but not all of them.

"Molly, give me a break, he only went because Notre Dame didn't take him," Keith said, and then raised his hands innocently when Audrey glared at him. "I'm not picking on her — she's the one that started it."

Patrick actually *was* crushed when he didn't get a football scholarship there — but he had three other scholarships waiting, so going into the Marines was his choice. "He went because he's patriotic," I said.

"He went because he's too dumb to understand what's going on over there," one of the other guys said. "Our government is the enemy in Vietnam, and now he's one of their little storm troopers."

They were calling Patrick a *Nazi*? For serving his country?!

Audrey had moved to stand in between us. "Why don't you guys just lay off? This is supposed to be a party, remember?"

"This war is *wrong*," Keith said to me. "And if it weren't for Patrick, you'd think so, too."

Would I? I don't even know. It's all so — complicated, and I'm not sure what's right. I'm not even sure there *is* a right answer. "I don't like wars, period," I said. "But I can think this war is wrong, and still support my brother. He's just trying to help."

"Oh, yeah," Jeff said. "Killing people helps a lot. That would sure make my family proud of *me*."

The argument went on from there, with more

people joining in and yelling a lot. As far as I could tell, no one changed their minds, and everyone ended up angry and confused. During the middle of all this, people in the living room suddenly started yelling, "10, 9, 8 . . ." and I realized that it was midnight.

It wasn't exactly a great way to start 1968.

January 2, 1968

My New Year's resolution is to *do* something. I guess I usually make dumb resolutions, like not eating so much chocolate, or not ever losing my temper — which always last about a week. It's so frustrating to know that you're only fifteen, and you don't have the power to change anything, and no one's really going to listen to you, anyway, because you're not old enough.

But I could still try.

I'm just not sure how to do it, and or even what to do. If I wanted to protest, I could go downtown and stand around Boston Common, holding signs with hippies, any day of the week. But even if I could get around the fact that it would be betraying Patrick, I don't think that really accomplishes anything. I've seen lots of demonstrators — especially over in Harvard Square — and I know I'm not supposed to say this, but it seems like a big waste of time to me. Everybody chants things like "Hey, hey, LBJ, how many kids did you kill today?" and people just walk right by without even noticing them. Besides, the government *knows* that lots of people are against the war, and they just keep asking for more troops, anyway.

When Lyndon Johnson first took over for President Kennedy, I thought he did a good job. He's in favor of civil rights, and helping the poor and the elderly and the sick. Those are all great things. But now it's just all about war. He said he'd never send Americans over there to fight another country's war — and he turned right around and did it. Everything would have been different if President Kennedy was still here — I'm sure of it. He wouldn't have let this happen.

God, that was a terrible day. I was in seventh grade, and we were just sitting in French class when our gym teacher came running in, crying. He said something to Mrs. Torrance, and then she got upset, too. None of us had ever seen adults do anything like that — in public — so we were already scared. I remember when she told us the President had been shot, Bobby O'Dowd said, "The president of *what?*" It made sense to me, but Mrs. Torrance was furious at him.

After she told us, a lot of people started crying. I think the whole country admired President Kennedy, but here in Boston, he was our *hero*. He was from here, he was Irish, he was Catholic. No one seemed to know what to do, and they ended up sending us home from school. When I was walking by the front office, I heard some teachers inside saying that Russia was going to attack us now, and no one would ever be safe again, and stuff like that.

That had *me* ready to cry, and when the teachers saw me, they closed the door so that I wouldn't be able to hear them talking anymore. I was still standing there, when Patrick came running up. He took my hand, and we walked around until we found a bunch of other kids who live in our neighborhood. Then Patrick called Mom, and said he was going to make sure everyone got home okay.

So, about ten of us walked home together. Patrick stopped at each house to make sure that the kid got inside, and that someone was home, and then we'd go to the next house. Grace Carter's parents weren't home, so we brought her back with us. Then, for the next four days, everyone just sat and stared at the television. We saw Lyndon Johnson speak as the new President, and then we saw that crazy man, Jack Ruby, shoot the *crazier* man, Lee Harvey Oswald, who shot the President. It was all right there — *on television.* To me, television was just supposed to be *I Love Lucy* and *Father Knows Best* and *The Ed Sullivan Show*, but now we were seeing people get *killed*, right in front of us. We watched the funeral, we watched Jackie Kennedy, and poor little Caroline and John-John, and none of it seemed real.

It was more than four years ago, and I still can't believe it happened. Sometimes it seems like before that day, everything was safe, and good — and ever since then, this country has been a scary place, where anything can happened. Like wars and riots and people killing each other. Since President Kennedy died, nothing has been the same, and now we're fighting a terrible war, ten thousand miles away. Maybe the thing I remember most is how terrible it was to see all of the grown-ups look so frightened. Even my father seemed scared, although he went off to work, as usual. If they were all afraid, how were *we* supposed to feel?

How should we feel now?

So, I know I want to do something. Something good. Something worthwhile. Something that makes a difference.

I'm just not sure what it should be.

January 3, 1968

These days, I wake up to the sound of my parents' alarm clock, down the hall. I always read until really late at night, so I have a hard time getting up in the morning. Usually my mother has to come in at least two or three times, to be sure I'm awake.

But, for some reason, that alarm clock ringing really jolts right through me lately. I guess because it's really hard to sleep since Patrick left, and I've been having a lot of bad dreams. So it's sort of a relief to wake up.

For years, the first sound I usually heard in the morning was the *thump* when Patrick rolled out of bed in the room next to mine and started doing push-ups. I'm not even sure he opened his eyes, first. Just *thud*, and you'd hear him counting. He always did at least two hundred, and then he would switch over to sit-ups.

He'd even do it out of season, except for Patrick, I don't think sports are ever out of season.

The only thump anyone hears coming from *my* room is if I drop the book I'm reading.

When he was home on leave, Patrick told me that when he got to Parris Island for boot camp, lots of the other guys were out of shape. Not Patrick. After graduation, while he was waiting to turn eighteen, he got this job on a loading dock. So, he'd spend the whole day lugging boxes and things around. Coach Ralston gave him a key to the school gym, so he could work out whenever he wanted. Then, when two-a-day practices started for the football team, Patrick went whenever he wasn't at work. And after *that*, he'd usually go run a few miles. So he said the physical part of boot camp wasn't bad at all, but that having all of the drill sergeants screaming at him, and not getting any sleep or being able to eat normal meals or anything was really tough. He also said that it should be tough, because the war was going to be a lot worse. And Dad would just nod, so I would never say anything.

But I really miss waking up to that *thump* every morning.

January 5, 1968

It's been good to be back at school this week. Christmas vacation gave me too much time to sit around and think, and worry. Compared to that, homework and tests don't seem that bad, even when the subjects are boring. Plus, I'm on Student Council, and I write for the newspaper and everything, so I have plenty to do. Our newspaper advisor, Mrs. Garson, is really uptight, though, and we're not allowed to write about anything that might be controversial. She doesn't even want us to express our opinions in editorials. Maybe I don't get it, but isn't that the whole point of having a school newspaper?

She only likes happy stories about things like the Pep Club and the band's bake sales and the latest basketball game. I try to write more interesting articles, but she either covers them with red pencil until there isn't much left, or just shakes her head, says *no*, and hands them back to me. She's always threatening to kick me off the staff, and once she even called my mother to complain. That was when I wrote a story about the way girls and boys are treated differently at my school. I only used facts — the way the guidance counselors encourage the boys to apply to college and tell lots of the girls to go to secretarial or beauty school, the way the dress code for us is twice as strict as the one for boys, and things like that — but Mrs. Garson just crumpled the story up. That made me really mad, and I had to leave the room before I said anything stupid. I had some great stuff in that story. Like I got a bunch of people to count the number of times boys were called on during their classes, and the number of times girls were. It turned out that the boys were getting to participate two or three times as much as the girls were. There's something really wrong with that, and it deserved to be in the school paper.

Actually, Mrs. Garson was my English teacher freshman year — and she didn't like me then, either. But she had to give me A's, because I always did my homework and studied for the tests. Most of the teachers at my school only seem to want you to just sit there quietly, do your work, and never express your opinion. So, they usually aren't crazy about me, and they're always saying things like "Why can't you be more like Brenda? She's such a lovely girl." Every time it happens again, I tell

Brenda about it, and she just laughs and says, "Yeah, *sure* I am."

I really hope things are different in college.

January 7, 1968

Theresa and Laurel and I went over to Harvard Square yesterday. Sometimes we ride our bikes, but since it's the middle of winter, we took the bus.

My father is always grumpy when he hears we're going there. "Off to see the hippies again?" he asks.

"Beautiful People, Dad," I say. "It's much cooler to call them 'The Beautiful People.'"

"Oh, yeah, real beautiful," he says, and goes back to reading the paper.

I think Harvard Square is fantastic. It's crowded, and noisy, and full of fun stuff to do. There's always a demonstration of some kind going on, and wherever you look, you see college students and just regular kids hanging out. Sometimes, the sidewalks are so crowded, that people spill right over into the streets and don't even pay attention to the cars trying to get through. It always feels like a big celebration to me. Everyone's really young, and because of Harvard and Radcliffe being right there, you know that you're surrounded by a lot of people who are really *smart*. I like that.

And, of course, there are the hippies. (Some of them are probably smart, but I don't think it's their top priority.) The Beautiful People. Peaceniks. Flower children. They wear lots of bright colors, super-tight pants, long hair, bangle bracelets, high-heeled boots, and really funky hats. People are holding hands, playing guitars, singing, and giving you peace signs when you walk by. Or they're playing chess, selling handmade jewelry, camping out right there on the street, and sometimes even begging for money. There are all these neat smells drifting through the air — incense, patchouli, sandalwood, curry, candles, really strong coffee, old musty books. And there's music everywhere. Rock and roll, folk music, guitars, sitars, chimes — just this big jumble of sounds all mixed up.

It's like — I don't know — a carnival. My father says I'm just looking at the pretty parts, and not seeing the drug overdoses, the runaways, and what he calls "shiftless people." So? What's wrong with seeing the pretty parts? He's also always warning me not to accept anything to eat or drink from strangers, because I guess he assumes that the hippies' main goal in life is to try and lure kids into becoming drug addicts. Sounds pretty unlikely to me, but I'm not about to take a bite from some stranger's sandwich or drink out of their cup, anyway, because — well, let's face it, I don't know where they've been. I wish he wouldn't say stuff like that in front of my mother, though. She worries enough, without him adding to it like that.

But if she's not around, I always ask my father stuff like, "Dad, what if a shiftless person says, 'Hey, little girl, want some candy?' What do I do?"

The only answer I've ever gotten is that if a shiftless person offers me candy, he wants to *hear* about it.

Anyway, back to Harvard Square. Looking at all of the people is entertaining enough, but there are also streets jammed with great little stores and diners and tiny restaurants. You can get neat secondhand clothes and jewelry at the thrift shops, although, okay, I like the bookstores the best. There are bookstores on just about every block. I usually come home with a whole stack of used paperbacks, for maybe ten cents each, and you can find these really interesting, radical anti-war magazines like *Ramparts* at the newsstand. If there were *pro*-war magazines, I would read them, too, just to try and understand both sides. But — that's definitely not the sort of reading material you find in Harvard Square.

I like seeing the buttons everyone wears, too, pinned to their jackets or floppy hats. Some of them just have peace signs. I bought one, but I haven't decided whether Patrick would be upset if I wore it. I'll ask, the next time I write him. Some of the buttons are pretty funny. They say things like: "END POVERTY, GIVE ME $10." Or "I'M TRYING TO FIND MYSELF. HAVE YOU SEEN ME ANYWHERE?" Or "IS THERE INTELLIGENT LIFE ON EARTH?" A couple of the boys at school who are completely obsessed by that dumb show *Star Trek* wear pins like that. Some of the other buttons are more angry, like I saw one that said, "CAUTION: MILITARY SERVICE MAY BE HAZARDOUS TO YOUR HEALTH." Or: "NAPALM MAKES MILLIONAIRES." "SAVE LIVES, NOT FACE." And there are plenty that just say "FLOWER POWER" or have drawings of doves, or a black hand and a white hand clasped together. Plus, there are the buttons from various peace marches in Washington, D.C., New York, and San Francisco.

46

We usually stop at a coffeehouse like Tulla's or Club 47, and listen to folk music, and try to look older. I don't like folk music much — okay, I can't stand it — but it feels pretty cool to make the scene with a bunch of college kids.

My friend Laurel is really into Joan Baez and Bob Dylan, so she could spend all day listening to folk singers. Good folk singers, bad folk singers — she doesn't care. She's been teaching herself to play the guitar and she's starting to write her own songs, too. One day, she'll probably be up there performing. Theresa had been taking classical piano lessons for as long as I've known her, so I don't think she's too crazy about folk music, either. But we all like the coffee. I put more sugar in mine than I think you're supposed to, but it tastes better that way.

Yesterday at Tulla's, there weren't too many singers, but a bunch of shaggy-haired people were taking turns standing up in front of each other and reading poetry. I'm not what you would call a poetry expert, but when someone keeps rhyming "free" and "be" and "the beauty of the sea," I'm probably not going to get up and shout "Bravo!" and ask them to read more.

The strange part is that so many other people did.

"Look at me; I climbed the tree," I said to Theresa and Laurel, really quietly.

Theresa laughed, but Laurel was a little offended.

"I thought he was good," she said.

"You thought he was cute," Theresa said.

Then, Laurel laughed, too. "Okay. Yeah."

The coffee was swell, though. Honestly.

January 10, 1968

I went over to Brenda's house to babysit this afternoon. I usually go there at least twice a week, to give her some time off — and me a chance to play with Jane and Gregory. She says she loves being a mother, and it's what she always wanted, but I still think she must need a little break, sometimes.

Gregory is just starting to walk, so I spend a lot of time chasing him around. He seems to be on a mission to find as much trouble as possible, so he does things like drink out of the dog's water bowl. Gregory takes after Hank's side of the family, since he's very blond.

And he's really big for his age, so I guess he takes after Hank there, too.

Or maybe not, since I'm the only short one in our family. Brenda and my mother are both about five-seven, and so far, I can't even get past five-two. Since Jane's tall and skinny for a three-year-old, maybe she'll even pass me one of these days.

There's a scary thought. Having to look *up* at your little niece?

So, Brenda took off for a couple of hours, and I didn't ask her where she was going. I mean, it's her free time, right? And my mother's only about a mile away, if God forbid, there was any sort of problem with the kids, and I had to call for advice — or help.

Between chasing Gregory and trying to get him interested in playing with some of his trucks and blocks, Jane and I drew pictures and squeezed clay into weird shapes. Jane thought that was pretty hilarious. Then I fixed Gregory some milk, while Jane and I drank juice and ate a couple of vanilla wafers apiece. So far, Jane seems like a Flaherty all the way. Same sort of sense of humor, same way of suddenly getting really intense out of nowhere and staring you straight in the eye. I don't think I ever realized that I did that — that we all do — until I saw her doing it, and it just looked so familiar. Sort of like looking in a mirror.

Brenda came home just as I was trying to figure out how to make supper, and watch two wildly energetic little kids, at the same time. I wasn't doing a very good job of it, either. She had a bag of groceries in each arm, and was also carrying a stack of mail. I could see an air-mail envelope on top.

"Patrick?" I asked, and she nodded.

We didn't get a chance to read it until the groceries were unpacked, the kids had eaten supper, and Brenda was giving them a bath. I sat down on the floor to read the letter aloud. I figured it was safe to read even if Jane and Gregory were halfway paying attention, because Patrick and I made a deal before he left. We agreed that if he wanted to write about anything really bad, but didn't want to upset the rest of the family, he would mail it to Theresa's house, instead. Luckily, it hasn't happened so far. I figure that every day that Theresa doesn't tell me that she got a letter is another day when things are going okay for Patrick.

I try to ignore the fact that it takes at least a week, and usually ten days, for his letters to get here. That means that any letter we get from him is old news, and in the meantime, all sorts of things could have happened to him.

Except that I promised not to think that way.

So, Patrick's letter. He started off with: *"Dear Brenda, Hank, Jane and — what's the little one's name again?"*

I thought that was funny; Brenda said, "Hmmm."

The letter was pretty similar to the ones my parents and I have gotten during the last couple of days. He and his company have been transferred out to guard a hill near the main base of Khe Sanh. It's called Hill 881S, and unfortunately, Mr. Trabowsky at the post office was right — there *were* some really bad fights out there last spring. I went back and looked at old *Life* and *Time* magazines, until I found the stories. I hope that area is safe now — it's hard to tell much from what Patrick's writing. Mostly, he says they're busy "digging in," which means digging foxholes and making bunkers. And he seems to be making some good friends, because he's started mentioning people by name. Or, more accurately, by nickname. Bebop, Hollywood, the Professor, Mooch. I was surprised that he wasn't using their real names — Joe, Ted, Bill, whatever — but my father says that's pretty common in the service. In World War II,

Dad's nickname was "Moose," because he's really tall and broad-shouldered. Patrick says that at first they were all calling him "Boston," which he didn't really like, but now his nickname is "Mighty Mouse." He thinks he was probably better off with "Boston," but — too late now.

He says they drank some canned eggnog on New Year's Eve, and fired flares into the air at midnight.

He also drew some pictures on the back of the second page for Jane and Gregory, but I waited to show them until they were out of their bath, because they were splashing so much. One picture was of him, standing on a very tall hill, waving. Brenda checked first to make sure he hadn't drawn a gun or anything — but Patrick knows better than that. There was a sketch of Brenda and Hank's dog, Bud (who I found up near Coolidge Corner last year, near the movie theater), and one of a very strange-looking bird he had seen. Brenda and I couldn't decide if the actual *bird* was odd — or if Patrick just isn't a very good artist. A little of both, probably. Jane and Gregory were enthusiastic, though.

Jane wanted to know when Uncle Patrick would come and bring her a present.

Brenda and I just looked at each other, and then Brenda said, "Before you know it, sweetie."

While I was waiting for Mom to come pick me up — boy, it will be great when I can actually drive my-self — Brenda and I sat in the kitchen, drinking Cokes.

"I think he's okay," I said, "don't you?"

"Oh, definitely," Brenda agreed. "He sounds fine."

But we didn't really look at each other this time.

January 14, 1968

The Super Bowl was on today, so my parents invited a bunch of people to come over to watch it. Relatives, firefighters, the usual. We had Cokes and beer and potato chips and spaghetti, and lots of casseroles and cookies that my aunts and a couple of the firefighters' wives brought. Of course, football made all of us think even more about Patrick, but nobody said much about it, other than to ask how he was doing and if they could read some of his letters.

I know they have radios in Vietnam, because Patrick has mentioned it. I wonder if they'll get to listen to some of the game? Dad says that Armed Forces Radio tries to play important sporting events for the soldiers. I hope so. Right before he left, Patrick was joking that he wished they had waited to send him overseas until after the football season, but that at least he'd been able to watch the Red Sox in the World Series for the first time in our lives. The fact that they lost in seven games didn't make the season — or our favorite player, Carl Yastrzemski — any less great. How can you not love a team that goes from ninth place to first place in just one season?! (Actually, we still loved them when they were in ninth place.)

I had trouble concentrating on the football game, but I watched and took notes, so that I'd be able to write Patrick a good description of it. Dad's still sending him lots of articles from the newspapers, too. Naturally, we root for the Boston Patriots, but Patrick will watch *any* football game, anytime, anywhere.

So the living room feels just that much more empty without him here today.

Later —

The Green Bay Packers won. The score was a little bit closer than the actual game, because the Packers were in control all the way. Patrick likes their quarterback, Bart Starr — and completely admires their coach, Vince Lombardi — so I'm sure he'll be glad when he hears that they won.

My Uncle Jim maybe did a little too much "celebrating" at the party, and during halftime, he started telling jokes. They were pretty harmless at first, but then he made some cracks about black people that really bothered me. More than a couple of the other men laughed — but, to my father's credit, his only reaction was to frown and instantly look over at me.

I thought about not saying anything — Uncle Jim tends to run at the mouth, although he's basically a big teddy-bear type. But, if you just walk away, isn't that almost as bad as actually making the joke in the first place?

My father must have given my mother a heads-up, because she suddenly appeared in the kitchen doorway.

"Molly, would you mind coming in here to help me with something?" she asked.

I got halfway across the room, before I had to stop because Uncle Jim had just told an even worse joke.

"Uncle Jim, would you mind not saying things like that?" I asked. "It really bothers me."

He stopped laughing and looked confused, instead. "Saying things like what?"

"Jokes about another race of people," I said.

He laughed, and took this really dramatic deep breath. "Oh, God, looks like I'm in for it now."

"Molly, let it go," my Uncle Colin said quietly. "He doesn't mean anything by it."

No, he probably didn't. Uncle Jim is a nice man. A *really* nice man. He just — says a lot of stupid stuff. I didn't want to make a scene and ruin the party for everyone else, so maybe it was enough just to make my point and then go help my mother.

Except for one thing.

"Uncle Jim, what color were those children you rescued last week?" I asked him. He had crawled through a burning apartment in Dorchester until he found them huddling in a corner, and he managed to get all three of them out safely, just before the whole room went up in flames. It was really heroic, and he'd gotten his picture in the paper and everything.

He looked at me blankly. "What do you mean?" Then, even though he was definitely pretty tipsy, he figured it out. "Oh. Well, they were Negroes."

"If you'd known that before you went in there,

would you still have risked your life to try and rescue them?" I asked.

Now everyone in the room stared at me.

"Of course," my uncle said, as if I were a total idiot. "What do you think?"

What *did* I think? "Just making sure," I said, and then — to my mother's visible relief — I went into the kitchen.

Uncle Jim is an incredibly brave man. A very thoughtful man. And a man who sometimes says terrible things not only about black people, but all minorities — and women, too.

How can you make sense of that?

I was really glad when the game ended and everyone went home. I stayed in the kitchen until the fourth quarter, when I finally came out, feeling really self-conscious. But Uncle Jim patted the couch next to him and — since it seemed like the best choice — I sat there for the rest of the game. And, other than harrassing the referees whenever he thought they made a bad call, he didn't tell any more jokes.

Boy, I'm tired.

Dad just took Maggie out for her late walk, but then she came running to my room and jumped onto my bed. She had a biscuit, which she ate, wagging her tail the whole time, and then she was asleep about ten seconds later. It must be fun to be a dog.

After I finished the homework that had been lying around all weekend, I read one of my parents' most recent issues of *Newsweek*, and it made me feel even more depressed. The cover story was about the war, and there was a picture of these really young, injured soldiers in the middle of the jungle someplace.

I wonder about photographers sometimes. You always see so many awful pictures of things — wars, fires, accidents, whatever — and I can't imagine how someone could just stand there taking pictures of tragedies, instead of dropping their cameras and running over to try and help. I guess they're just trying to report the stories to the rest of the world, but still, there's something really creepy about it. I mean, would my father stop to take pictures of a burning building before he ran inside? Not a chance. He would just go. Don't photographers ever have thoughts like that?

The cover article in *Newsweek* said that there are almost half a million American troops in Vietnam right now, and mostly the articles seemed to be making the argument that our being there was a good thing, and that the war should continue. Some of the leaders they interviewed disagreed, but it sure sounded like as far as Vietnam is concerned, we aren't going anywhere anytime soon. There was a good map, though, showing where all of our troops are, and I cut it out. Khe Sanh wasn't listed, but I marked it in, right below the DMZ, on the far left.

It really looks lonely up there.

January 15, 1968

I got sent to the office today for "espousing Communist ideology." Espousing. You don't hear *that* word every day. I looked it up, just to make sure I knew what it meant. I assumed it had something to do with being in favor of Communism, and I was right — it means you are loyal to, or support, something. All I did was ask my history teacher a couple of questions in class, and I ended up with detention and an appointment to see Mr. Moretti, the vice principal. Trudy Kravatz brought up Vietnam, when we were talking about the Civil War, and Mr. Hilder went off into his long rant about how America has to "stop the forces of Communist aggression," and how evil Communism is, and all of the usual stuff adults say about the war.

I'm getting really tired of always hearing the same arguments without any explanations, so I raised my hand and asked why Communism is so bad. Mr. Hilder's face got all red — he doesn't really like me, anyway, I don't think — and he gave us another version of "Communism is evil and must be stopped at all costs." And I said, okay, but as far as I understood it, the idea of Communism was that there weren't any class differences, so that everyone is all together in one big group and completely equal — and what was so bad about that? Some people in the class looked really curious, some of them were glaring at me, and — big shock — everyone else was just really bored and waiting for the bell to ring.

Then, I made things worse by asking if we were over there fighting Communism because we honestly think it's a bad thing — or because the United States just wants everyone to be exactly like us, because we think we know best. What if the Vietnamese people want to be Communists? I mean, maybe they do. I don't know, but did anyone ever *ask* them? I've read in magazines that life in Vietnam is centered around their villages and growing rice, and a lot of people spend their whole lives without ever going more than five miles away from where they were born. So, what if they don't want any form of government at all, except for maybe a village leader? Shouldn't they be allowed to do that? Maybe they don't like Democracy.

Mr. Hilder looked like he was about to explode, but he's a teacher, and we ought to be able to ask questions. Isn't it his job to answer them?

Right around then, this guy Lumpy, who's on the football team, jumped up and started yelling at me and saying I was being a traitor to my brother. I told him I was only asking because I want to know that my brother is over there risking his life for a good reason. Lumpy just punched his desk with his fist and kept yelling.

Then, Jason — Jason! — said that it was disloyal to Patrick and the country to talk like that, and Cathy Watkins, who was sitting next to him, said, "Yeah, *really*." All I could think was, oh, please, and I saw Theresa roll her eyes, too.

But a couple of other people started jumping up and saying stuff about how America is always right — except maybe when we aren't right, but that Communists are always wrong, and — it just went on and on. Before things could get even more out of control, Mr. Hilder ordered me to go down to the office, and said he would be down to "deal with me" after class.

I ended up sitting there for a long time, before he showed up. I've been sent to the office before — the last time was when I was part of the dress code protest in November, when all of the girls wanted to change the rules so that we would be allowed to wear pants to school, if we want. Especially in the winter, when it's *cold* out there. The only result was that we were sent home immediately to change out of our slacks and into "appropriate school garments," and all eleven of us got three days of detention. (Almost every girl in the school was in favor of changing the dress code, but not that many people ended up having the nerve to actually show up in pants and hold a sit-down in the main corridor.) My father was really upset, said he was embarrassed to have a daughter who didn't know how to be ladylike, and I got grounded for two weeks. My mother had more of a quiet "please just go along to get along" reaction.

I didn't agree with either of them. I still don't.

Anyway, when the secretaries saw me come into the office, they assumed I was just there to deliver a message or something. They're all really nice, and I like stopping by to talk to them sometimes when I have a free period, or a pass to go to the lavatory or something. I always figure that if you have a hall pass, there's no point in rushing back to class. You might as well take advantage of it.

"Hi," I said. "I got sent down to see Mr. Morelli."

They all seemed disappointed — mostly because they know I'm a really good student, and A students aren't supposed to cause trouble, I guess. But they were also ready to be amused, since they figured I wasn't down here for throwing food in the cafeteria or vandalizing the library or something.

"What did you do?" Miss Briggs asked, and I could hear the "this time" in her voice.

I know I'm supposed to show respect to my elders — my parents have pretty much hammered that into me — but did Mr. Hilder earn that respect today? Not if you ask me. "I just found out I'm a Communist," I said.

The secretaries — and Mrs. Creighton, the school nurse — all tried to look disapproving, but I could tell that most of them wanted to laugh.

"Take a seat, please, Molly," Mrs. Berman, who's in charge of the office, said, trying to sound stern.

I wanted to pick up a folding chair and politely ask

where they wanted me to put it — but I decided not to push my luck. So, I sat down next to two ninth-grade boys who had been fighting during gym class. Dodge ball turned ugly, I guess. They were still wearing shorts and T-shirts, and one of them had a bloody nose. Mrs. Creighton brought him an ice pack, and told him to tip his head back. The other kid just sulked, said his stomach hurt, and how come *he* couldn't have an ice pack? So, Mrs. Creighton got another ice pack. I started to raise my hand, as if I were going to ask for one, too, but she just grinned, shook her head, and went back to her office.

When Mr. Hilder finally showed up, I had already missed fourth period, and was worried about missing fifth period, because I had a chemistry test. He went straight back to Mr. Morelli's office, and they called me in about ten minutes later. I really like Mr. Morelli. He's strict, but he also has twinkly eyes. As far as I can tell, he generally gets a kick out of me, even when I'm being a jerk. He always liked Brenda and Patrick, too — although they got in a lot less trouble then I do.

Mr. Morelli folded his hands and looked across his desk at me. "So, Molly, what do you have to say for yourself?"

I had to take a deep breath and count to ten, because I had this really wild urge to shout something like "I defy all capitalist imperialists and pledge allegiance to the Tsar!"

I would have thought that was funny — but maybe this wasn't the right time.

"Mr. Hilder and I had a disagreement about boundaries," I said. "I apologize if I offended him."

Mr. Morelli looked pleased, since I think he'd expected me to pop off a smart remark. Mr. Hilder looked annoyed — probably for the same reason. It's a lot harder to stay mad at someone who's being polite, I guess.

"She agitated the entire class," he said stiffly.

What a terrible crime.

In the end, they decided that I would have two days of detention — because Mr. Hilder apparently wasn't going to be happy unless I got punished. He also said that I had to hand in a five-hundred word essay tomorrow about democracy and what it means to be an American.

I just kept saying things like "Yes, sir," "Absolutely, sir," and "I certainly will, sir." Sure thing. You bet. Can do.

The bell rang, and Mr. Hilder went off to his next class. I was hoping that I could leave, too, because I really didn't want to show up late to my chemistry test.

"So," Mr. Morelli said.

I sighed. "History has always been my favorite subject, sir."

"And it still should be," he said. "It's just that not everyone is comfortable with — lively discussions — these days."

No. Apparently not.

January 16, 1968

It took forever to write my essay on democracy last night, but I handed it in first thing this morning. It was very patriotic — and said absolutely nothing worthwhile. Theresa's advice had been to write the way a Miss America candidate would. It sounds silly, but that actually made it easier.

At supper last night, my father was all mad at me. He talked a lot about how I was going to ruin my chances for a college scholarship if I had a bad disciplinary record. He went on like that for a while, until my mother suddenly looked up and said, "*Enough*, Sean." My father was going to argue some more — the Flahertys almost never know when to quit — but then he just sat back and asked me to pass him the potatoes.

For the second day in a row, I was the only girl sitting in detention. Most of the guys there seemed to think that was sort of cool, but we weren't allowed to talk or anything. We just had to sit there for an hour and a half. That would have been fine — even fun — if we had been allowed to read, but anything other than sitting quietly was against the rules. So, we sat. And sat. And sat.

Just as detention was finally ending, my history teacher from last year, Mrs. Jorgensen, came in. She always used to give me an extra reading list, so that I could go to the library — or the bookstores in Harvard Square — and find out more about whatever we were studying at the time. Which I just about always did, except when we were studying the Tudor period in England, which I thought was pretty boring.

Maybe Mr. Hilder would be glad to know that while I might be a Communist, I'm not that big on the monarchy.

Mrs. Jorgensen sat down in the desk next to mine. She's probably the best teacher I've ever had at this school, and I hope I get her again next year. "There have been some interesting discussions in the Teacher's Room today," she said.

Maybe my father's right, and I *am* going to have trouble finding people to write college recommendations for me.

I could tell she was waiting for me to answer, and I tried to think of something halfway intelligent to say. "Everyone always says that Communism is bad, but no one ever tells us *why*," I said finally. "I was reading a little about it, and it sounded pretty good. I mean, if you had a society that was really equal — you know, no rich people, no poor people — wouldn't things like segregation and prejudice go away?"

Instead of getting mad, she just looked thoughtful — which is why she's a good teacher. "Well, on paper, it *does* make some sense, Molly," she said. "But, in reality, it never seems to work out that way, because inevitably some people would rather be in charge than have total equality. Then it tends to turn into fascism."

I may read a lot, but all of those "isms" confuse me. Communism, socialism, fascism, totalitarianism, Marxism, Leninism . . . I'm going to have to read more about them.

"Do you think we're doing the right thing by being over there?" I asked. "In Vietnam, I mean? Or is the war just making things worse for them?"

She thought that over. "I honestly have no idea," she said.

January 20, 1968

I went over to Theresa's house this morning, because we were planning to go to a matinee. She wanted to go see *Casablanca* over at the theater in Harvard Square. I've seen it about four times, but I really like it, so I would have been happy to go. But I was trying to talk her into going downtown instead to see *Camelot* again. Yeah, I like rock and roll, but the truth is, I'd usually rather listen to the soundtrack from a musical. Patrick has always made fun of me whenever he's caught me listening to *The King and I* or *The Fantastiks* or something — but he can't have hated it that much, since he knows all of the words to the songs, too.

I've used that little piece of information for brotherly blackmail, more than once.

Theresa was still practicing one of her piano concertos

when I got to her house, so I sat down in an easy chair to wait. She wants to apply to Juilliard next year to study music, and she's spending this whole year working on pieces for her audition. I really don't know much about playing instruments — no one in my family has any talent at all; we don't even clap our hands very well — but she sure sounded good to me. I don't think she felt the same way, though, because every so often she would mutter something and start a passage all over again.

"That was great," I said when she finished.

Theresa made a face and sat down on the couch across from me. "Not really," she said. "But thanks."

Her mother had made some meatball sandwiches and cole slaw for us, and we went out to the kitchen to eat. If you ask me, Mrs. Garofano is probably the best cook in the world. Theresa opened the newspaper to the movie listings, so we could check and see what else was playing. I thought *Dr. Doolittle* might be fun, but she didn't look too excited about the idea, and we were back to deciding between *Casablanca* and *Camelot*.

"Have your parents changed their minds about the animal shelter yet?" she asked.

I've been trying to convince them for a couple of

weeks that it would be really great if I could volunteer there. So far, they just keep saying absolutely not, because they're afraid I'll bring home too many pets, and they think four is enough. My mother wants me to go be a candy striper at St. Elizabeth's Hospital, instead. My Aunt Kelley works there, and could set it up for me, and it's also right around the corner from the high school. But, I don't know, the idea of spending time in a hospital just sounds so grim.

"Not so far," I said. "Mom says I can come help her at the Rosary and Altar Society, if I want." That's the women's group at St. Anthony's, which does stuff like raise money and decorate the church for the holidays.

"Yuck," Theresa said.

Double yuck. I was really disappointed that they kept saying no about the animal shelter, because I had thought that it would be the perfect place for me. I could be doing something good — and something I liked — at the same time.

Except that I probably *would* fall in love with all of the strays.

"Maybe I should just be a hippie," I said.

Theresa shook her head. "I don't think so. You'd have to be mellow."

Oh. Whoa. Mellow would be hard for me.

"There'd be all of that folk music, too," Theresa pointed out.

Okay. Too horrifying for *me*.

We were sitting there eating oatmeal cookies, and trying to decide if this would make us fat, when Theresa's mother came in with the mail.

"Well, isn't this nice," she said, and smiled at me. "Your brother sent Theresa a letter."

Theresa and I both sat up really straight, since we both knew that that only meant one thing — he was sending me a letter he didn't want my parents to see. Mrs. Garofano plopped down cheerfully at the table, so that she could listen to whatever Patrick had to say. Without even having to look at each other, Theresa and I were trying to figure out a way to stall, but then luckily, the phone rang. Once Mrs. Garofano was deep in conversation, we escaped to Theresa's room to read the letter privately.

Since I don't want to show it to my parents, I'm going to keep the letter — and any others he sends — here in my diary, where it'll be safe. This is what he wrote:

Dear Molly,

I hope you're doing okay. I don't want to upset you or any-thing, but you're the person I always talk to about stuff that bothers me, and — you don't mind, right? Because something really bad happened yesterday, and I miss you, and I wish I could talk to you.

I know I've written to all of you about my buddy Holly-wood. The really funny guy, with all of the girlfriends? He got killed yesterday. I really want to cry — but you just can't over here. Bebop (you remember which one he is, right? My friend from Detroit who plays the saxophone?) and I were putting some barbed wire out in front of our position, and most of the rest of the guys were behind us working on our trenches. There was this big explosion, and — Molly, Hollywood was all blown up. I'm not sure I should even tell you this, but his legs were gone, and he was talking *to me. Then he died, while I was still hold-ing his hand. I was looking right at him, and he just* died.

I really do want to cry. I want to cry a lot. (Promise you won't tell anyone.) He was such a good guy.

I'm not on the hill right now. (Don't tell Mom and Dad this, either.) Bebop and I got pretty cut up by the razors on the barbed wire, so we got sent down here to the medical aid sta-tion on the main Khe Sanh base. Don't worry — we're okay.

A few stitches, no big deal. I'm writing this really fast, because Bebop's still getting his arm sewn up, and I don't want him to know how freaked out I am.

It's scary here. I'm scared every day and, especially, at night, when I'm on guard. We spend all our time just waiting for something bad to happen, and — it really gets to you. Then something bad actually did *happen, and — I can't even think. It was just too awful. But I know I have to pull it together and be a tough guy, because that's my job. No one ever talks about being scared, so I might be the only one. And I would* never *want the other guys to know I feel this way. Or that I get really bad headaches, and sometimes my stomach hurts so much I have trouble eating.*

I'm not sure I'm going to mail this, because I'm afraid it'll upset you. But it makes me feel better to tell you, and I know you'll be cool about it. Just make sure Mom and Dad don't see this. Especially Mom. Or Brenda, either.

If you don't want me to send you stuff like this, let me know, okay? And I promise I won't do it again.

Okay, here comes Bebop — I have to go now.

Love, Patrick

After I read the letter, I showed it to Theresa, because I know Patrick trusts her not to tell anyone, either, so he wouldn't mind. Neither of us knew what to say, but my stomach and head had definitely started hurting.

"He's going to be okay," Theresa said. "He just needed to tell someone about it."

The only time I've ever seen Patrick scared is when Dad was in the hospital after a ceiling collapsed on him while he was fighting a fire in Chinatown. And that was more than eight years ago, so we were both pretty young. I read the letter again, and almost started crying.

"What can I do to help him?" I asked. "He sounds so — I just want to help."

When Theresa looked at me, she seemed a lot older than sixteen — which is one of the things I like best about her. "You can keep reading these letters when he sends them to you," she said.

Right. I can do that. And I will do that — although I hope to God that he never has to write another one.

We never did end up going to the movies.

January 21, 1968

Khe Sanh has been attacked. *Attacked.*

Mom and I were watching the news, and eating

supper on TV trays, because Dad was at work. Since he's the company captain, he pulls a lot of extra tours, and works double-shifts pretty often. We were only half paying attention, because we were really waiting for *F-Troop* to come on. And I was telling her all about my Drama Club meeting, and how I wanted us to do *A Streetcar Named Desire* for our spring play, but everyone else was voting for either *Our Town* or *Guys & Dolls*. Since I think there are only about two guys in the whole school who would be willing to get up and sing in public, I don't think *Guys & Dolls* is going to work.

Then we heard Walter Cronkite say "Khe Sanh." He was reporting that the base at Khe Sanh came under heavy attack early this morning (except that because of the International Dateline, it's already tomorrow there) by the North Vietnamese Army. Hundreds, and maybe thousands, of rockets and mortar rounds hit the base, a lot of Marines were injured and killed, and the ammunition dump blew up, causing a massive explosion.

My mother was absolutely frozen in her chair, gripping her coffee mug with one hand. There weren't many details beyond that, and no film of the attack, but "military sources" were quoted as saying they thought it was the beginning of a major offensive by the enemy.

"They didn't say anything about the hills, Mom," I said. "I'm sure he's okay."

She just stared at the television — and I did, too.

January 24, 1968

The news reports get worse and worse. Khe Sanh is under daily attack, and the headlines in the newspaper say things like "Reds Target Khe Sanh; Marines Under Siege." "Reds" are what they call Communists. Yesterday, we read that one of the hills near the base was attacked and almost overrun by a battalion of NVA soldiers. The article said it was Hill 861, and we checked and double-checked Patrick's letters to make sure that his hill was called 881S, not 861.

It's really scary to keep hearing about these attacks, while the letters we're getting from Patrick are more than a week old. I haven't told my parents about the one he sent me about his friend dying — and I'm definitely not going to do it now. His latest letter to all of us just talks about them going on routine patrols, and how heavy all of his gear is to carry. Other than that, he mentioned that there were more fighter jets flying past his hill lately, and he thanked us for the latest box of cookies, and iced-tea mix, and other stuff we sent him.

Mom's a wreck, and is spending twice as much time over at St. Anthony's than she usually does. Brenda is coming over more than usual. Having Jane and Gregory running around the house is such a nice distraction for everyone. Other than that, all we can do is wait for the news to come on, and pray that we *don't* get an official United States Marine Corps telegram.

Father McDougal, our parish priest, came over for supper tonight, which I think made my mother feel a little better. But it got on my nerves, because even though he's a nice man, I don't want to hear anything about the will of God, or the wisdom of a higher power being beyond our understanding. Once the conversation headed in that direction, I excused myself and went out to the kitchen to start doing the dishes.

A few minutes later, Father McDougal came in. He's in his late fifties, with gray hair and glasses. Even though she'd already greeted him repeatedly, Maggie jumped up from a sound sleep on the floor and wagged her tail wildly. Father McDougal patted her, and remarked about "what a fine-looking dog she is." I thanked him, and kept washing dishes. I was hoping that he would leave, but instead he picked up a kitchen towel and started drying plates.

"Your brother's a very brave young man," he said.

I certainly wasn't going to disagree with *that*.

"Your mother's faith comforts her a great deal," he said. "I hope Patrick's comforts him."

I doubt it. Neither of us have ever been sure what we believe, and lately, I'm not even sure if I believe in God. Well, no — I still believe in God. I'm just not sure if he's merciful and kind, and all those other good things we were taught in catechism class.

"Does your faith help *you?*" Father McDougal asked.

Did he want an honest answer? Did he want to know that I'd been having doubts for years? That I feel pretty lousy about a world where Presidents get assassinated, black people get shot just for trying to vote, and American boys are fighting and dying *right this very minute*, ten thousand miles away from here? "No, Father, it doesn't," is all I said.

"Would you like to talk about it?" he asked. "Maybe I can help you find a way to answer your questions."

I wish he could — but I think I'm on my own with this one.

January 26, 1968

I'm so glad today was Friday — I couldn't concentrate at all on schoolwork this week. I even completely forgot to study for my French test, so I probably flunked it. I also skipped out on both Student Council and my school newspaper meeting. Cathy Watkins has been wearing Jason's varsity track jacket all over the place — and I don't even care. I just — I don't know. It's really hard to sleep at night, and I'm walking around filled with so much dread every minute, that I can't seem to think about anything else.

Theresa and Laurel and Dorothy Chamberlain asked me if I wanted to go over and hang out in Harvard Square this afternoon, and I just said thanks, but I couldn't today. Theresa suggested that we go over to my house, instead, but I said that I'd promised to help my mother do some stuff, and they should just go on without me. Finally, they did, but none of them looked too happy about it.

The truth is that I was just too tired to go to Harvard Square, or to talk to people, or to pretend to be having a good time. I was on my way to the main exit when Mrs. Jorgensen stopped me.

"Oh, Molly, I'm glad I saw you," she said, and

reached into her pocketbook. "I wrote out a list of books you might want to read, and I wanted to give it to you."

I thanked her, and put the piece of paper into my book bag without looking at it.

"Everything okay?" she asked.

What was I going to say, that everything was just *spiffy*? I just said yes, thank you. But I could tell that she wasn't going to let me walk away, so I added that I was a little tired this week, because Patrick's stationed at Khe Sanh.

She looked really surprised — and kind of upset, too. "I'm sorry about that," she said. "How's he doing?"

"I don't know," I said. "We're just . . . waiting to hear."

And that just about says it all.

We're waiting.

January 30, 1968

Mom, Dad and I each got a letter from Patrick today — and we found out Brenda got one, too. They were all pretty much the same — very short, only saying that he was heading out on a big patrol in the morning, he's thinking about us, he misses us, and he loves us. They were all dated January 19th, which was right before the attacks started at Khe Sanh.

I didn't need anyone to tell me that he had written those letters because he was afraid something might happen to him, and — just in case — he was saying good-bye.

February 2, 1968

We've had the television on almost constantly for the past few days. Suddenly, there are huge battles going on all over Vietnam at the same time. A truce had been set up for the Vietnamese holiday, Tet (it's supposed to be as big as Christmas, Easter, and the 4th of July combined). But in the middle of the night, while everyone's guard was down, the Viet Cong and the North Vietnamese Army — VC and NVA — attacked military bases and cities all over South Vietnam. They even took over the American Embassy in Saigon for about six hours. If they can get into our embassy like that, then there can't be any place in South Vietnam that's safe. So, as far as I can tell, the war is just spinning out of control.

The list of towns and bases they attacked seems to go on forever. Saigon, Tay Ninh, Bien Hoa, Cam Ranh Bay, Nha Trang, Tuy Hoa, Qui Nhon, Chu Lai, Danang, Quang Tri, Dong Ha, Phu Bai . . . they're all on my map, and they're spread out all over the country. And if any of the reporters mention Khe Sanh, most of them say something vague like, oh, yeah, Khe Sanh is still getting hit by rockets and mortars every day, too.

For once, a lot of people were actually talking about Vietnam at school today. You'd think it would be a major topic of conversation all the time, especially since it's our generation that's being the most seriously affected. But it really doesn't come up much, and when it does, only a few people stand around arguing about it while everyone else just shrugs and changes the subject.

But today was different. It's hard to ignore the fact that the war has become so much more serious — literally overnight. I was surprised by how many people came up to me to ask how Patrick was doing, and if we'd heard from him, and if we were worried. But I was more surprised by how many people *didn't* come up to me, especially since I've known most of them since elementary school.

Right before sixth period, I was talking to Oliver Moore — he's on the football team — about Patrick's most recent letter, when Jason walked by on his way to English class. I know he overheard the conversation, because he paused for a few seconds, and then kept walking. The halls had cleared out pretty quickly, the way they always do after the bell rings. I watched him walk away, and — without giving it much thought — I caught up to him.

"Hey," I said.

He turned, looking kind of nervous. "I'm late. Okay?"

Since we were in the same class, obviously he knew that I was late, too. I looked at him, wondering why I'd wasted about a year and a half having a crush on this guy. Yeah, he was smart, and he was cute — but he wasn't actually very nice. And he wasn't funny, and he wasn't what you'd call charming these days.

"What happened to you, Jason?" I asked.

Now, he looked uneasy. "What do you mean?"

"All through elementary school, we were friends," I said. "Junior high, too. We used to go over to each other's houses, sit together in the cafeteria, the whole thing. We even went to each other's birthday parties. And now you can't take the trouble to say hi, how you doing?"

He shrugged. "I don't know."

He didn't know. Swell. It didn't seem worth it to try finishing the conversation, so I just headed towards our English class.

Patrick's right — the guy *is* a punk.

February 3, 1968

We've only gotten one other letter from my brother this week, and it just came this morning. I hope that only means the mail has slowed down, because of how crazy everything seems to be over there. The letter was pretty short, and the only time he really mentioned the war was when he said things were "heating up a little." Other than that, he just said that he was kind of tired, it had been incredibly foggy up on the hill lately, and not to worry about him.

So, all we know is that he was okay ten days ago. My father's response was to go back to bed — he'd worked an extra-long tour. My mother immediately started baking, so that we could get another care package ready for Patrick. And I took Maggie for a walk, and then watched *American Bandstand* for a while.

I'm noticing more and more that my parents and I are spending too much time going off by ourselves, instead of sitting around and talking. That can't be a good thing. But that's what we're doing.

Later on, my father drove me over to Brenda's on his way back to the firehouse. I had promised to babysit for Jane and Gregory tonight, so that Brenda could go to a wedding shower for one of her friends. It was easier than usual, since they both just took their baths and then fell asleep almost as soon as I put them to bed. I went in to check on them every so often, but they seemed to be just fine. Gregory cried a little once, because he's getting a new tooth, but after that, he went right back to sleep.

So I read the latest issue of *McCall's*, talked on the telephone with both Theresa and Laurel for a while, and then played a really quiet game of fetch with Bud. He got excited and barked a few times, but the noise didn't wake the kids up, luckily.

I was on the couch watching *Mannix* when Brenda

got home. Once she had looked in on the kids, she came back out to watch the end of the show with me. We'd already planned that I was going to spend the night, so that Mom wouldn't have to come out late to pick me up.

When the news came on, Brenda instantly turned it off.

"You don't want to see what's happening?" I asked.

"No," she said.

No?

"Molly, he has eleven more months over there," she said. "If we keep doing this to ourselves, we're all going to go around the bend."

I thought about that. "Crackers?" I asked.

"Wacko," she said.

We spent the next few minutes coming up with every word we could think of that meant "insane." It seemed pretty funny once we had gotten to phrases like "bats in the belfry" and "a few cards missing from the deck," and I ended up laughing for what was probably the first time in about two weeks.

"He doesn't want us moping around," Brenda said. "I mean, this is *Patrick*, remember? The goofball?"

Yeah, Patrick was definitely goofy. I told her about

the way Mom and Dad were all quiet, and how nervous it was making me. She sighed, and said that she and Hank were fighting twice as much as usual, and we were all just tense. That I shouldn't worry about it, because I was going to end up with an ulcer or something. She might be right, because I've been getting lots of stomachaches lately.

It was eleven-thirty now, and she turned the television back on. "I think we should make popcorn, and watch a movie," she said.

That sounded like a very cool plan.

We were watching a Jimmy Stewart movie when I remembered that I had forgotten to tell her that I had finally decided that Jason was kind of a jerk, and I wasn't going to think about him anymore.

Her answer was, "Took you long enough."

Hmmm. That's exactly what Theresa said.

February 5, 1968

I woke up this morning because I smelled smoke. It wasn't "Help, the house is on fire!" smoke; it was the smell of wet, smoky clothes. That meant my father was home. He was supposed to get off before the night tour yesterday, but one of his lieutenants had called in sick and he had to work straight through until this morning.

I went downstairs and found him sitting at the kitchen table with a full cup of coffee — and an empty bottle of Narragansett beer. He looked really tired, his hair was all matted, and he was still wearing his uniform.

I asked him if he was all right, and he nodded. So I asked him if Mom was already at morning Mass, even though it was so early, and he nodded again.

"You want me to make some breakfast?" I asked, and he shook his head.

We'd all seen Dad after so many bad fires over the years, that we had gotten really good at telling exactly how serious it had been just by looking at him. This one must have been unusually bad. His expression was so sad and distant that my first thought was that one of the other firefighters must have died. So I asked him if the guys were all okay, and he nodded and said, "Pretty much, yeah." Luckily. But that meant this one had involved civilians.

"How many?" I asked.

He let out his breath. "Nine."

Nine? No wonder he looked that way. "Children?" I asked, since that upsets firefighters more than anything else.

He shook his head. And I couldn't help thinking, thank God for that, at least. But I just sat down at the table, instead of asking him any more questions. If he wanted to tell me about it, he would. I think we sat there without talking for about ten minutes.

Finally, my father sighed. "It was one of those crummy residential hotels. The Roosevelt. Place went up like a Roman candle. Really juicy." "Juicy" is what the jakes say, when they describe a really hot, smoky, intense fire. "We had people hanging out of almost every window. So we were too busy pulling them out to get anyone up to open the roof right away, and —" He shook his head again.

When firefighters chop or saw holes in a roof, that lets out a lot of the smoke and heat, which makes it a lot safer for the jakes and civilians who are still inside the building. It's called ventilation. The firefighters from the ladder trucks usually do that, while the engine guys use their hoses to fight the fire.

"How many people did you get out?" I asked.

"I don't know," he said, still staring off at something I was glad I couldn't see. "About a hundred. Maybe a few more."

And that's the other thing about jakes. It's the ones they *don't* save that they remember, not the survivors.

There wasn't going to be anything I could say to make him feel better, but I found myself asking him if he was ever scared when he was at a big fire.

He just looked puzzled. "You mean, that I might lose one of my men?"

I'd meant being scared about *himself*, but it was pretty clear that the answer was no. "I think I'd be scared," I said.

He smiled a little, which I didn't expect at all, and reached down to pat Maggie on the head. "When you saw her running around in the street, did you worry about the traffic?"

"Well, yeah," I said. "I was afraid she might get hit."

"Were you afraid *you* might get hit?" he asked.

Oh. And the truth was that I couldn't remember that even crossing my mind. I was too busy trying to catch her.

My father smiled again. "You're a jake's daughter, Molly. It's in your blood, whether you like it or not."

Wow. What a neat thing to say.

I really hope he meant it.

February 10, 1968

Brenda's right — there's no way we can spend the rest of the year worrying ourselves sick. The news is still full of reports about what they're calling the Tet Offensive, except that so far, the enemy has lost every single battle. They're still fighting in a city called Hue, but other than that, the Offensive is pretty much over. So now, there are just two major stories. One is the latest piece of bad news — a U.S. Navy ship called the U.S.S. *Pueblo*, which was captured near North Korea. All of the sailors who were on board are now being held prisoner by the North Koreans, and for all I know, we're about to get into another war because of it.

And the other big story? Khe Sanh. It's being called the worst siege since Dien Bien Phu, which was a battle during the French-Indochina War. The French soldiers were completely surrounded by the North Vietnamese back in 1954 — and, in the end, they surrendered.

Now, our Marines are surrounded at Khe Sanh. There are only about five thousand of them, and at least twenty thousand NVA soldiers in the jungle around them. Maybe forty thousand. No one seems to know for sure. And on Patrick's little hill, there are only two hundred Marines, at the most. Surrounded by thousands. It's just horrible. The reporters are all using the same words to describe the situation. Besieged. Beleaguered. Desperate. And the one they keep hinting at is: *doomed*.

But, I just don't believe that. I mean, they're *Marines*. Marines hang tough. Marines fight back. At least that's the way Patrick sounds when he writes to us.

Only, if we have about half a million American troops in Vietnam, and it's that bad up there, why don't they just send in reinforcements?

Theresa has gotten two more letters for me so far, but it was easier for me to read them, now that I had more of an idea what to expect. In one, Patrick wrote about a really bad battle on the 20th, when he and his company went out to the hill just north of them, 881N. A bunch of Marines died, including his lieutenant and his platoon sergeant. About forty other people from his company were wounded badly enough to have been evacuated to hospitals. In his squad alone, they went from eleven guys, down to only five. I was glad to hear that his friends Bebop, Mooch, and the Professor were still with him. Those three, along with his friend Hollywood, are the ones he's always mentioned the most. Their squad machine gunner was wounded in action, so now Patrick is carrying what he calls "the pig," even though he'd never really fired one before. I guess in Vietnam, you have to learn on the job. He says it weighs about twenty-five pounds, so it must be a really big gun.

I can't stand guns.

The other letter was about the first day and night of the attacks at Khe Sanh. It was very different from the one he sent to the family, where he wrote repeatedly that we didn't have to worry, because the NVA's aim was lousy, and they all had good, solid bunkers to protect themselves on the hill. The one I got had a lot more details about how they had to watch the fight over on Hill 861 go on all night, and couldn't do anything to help except fire about eight hundred of their own mortar rounds over there to try and stop the waves of NVA soldiers attacking their fellow Marines. The main base had gotten pretty much flattened by NVA rockets and mortars the next day, and his hill had started getting hit, too. A lot of people he knows got hurt, and when the medevac helicopter came in to pick them up, the NVA shot it down, too. He referred to this as "a bad day."

Yeah. I'd say so.

The other thing I noticed? He doesn't sound scared anymore. He sounds *angry*. Which is probably a good thing, if it helps him get through this. I know he's protecting me from the worst details, but I'm glad that he feels he can tell me at least some of what's happening to him.

I wrote two letters back to him right away. One was really long and serious, and I made sure I let him know that I *wanted* him to keep sending me letters about *anything* he needed to tell someone. I kept the other one really brief. I didn't even write "Dear Patrick." All it said was: "I'm really worried about you — but is it okay if I don't go to early Mass *every* day?"

Patrick's one of the only people I know who might think that's funny.

February 12, 1968

I took the subway down to Park Street today, and then switched to the E Line, so I could ride out to Angell Memorial, Boston's biggest animal shelter and veterinary hospital. My mother wasn't home, so I just left her a note that said I was "around," and I'd be back in time for supper. I hope she doesn't remember that I was supposed to be at my newspaper meeting after school, since she might get suspicious.

The subway ride was pretty long — up past Northeastern University, and then over onto South Huntington Avenue. My parents weren't going to be happy about this, but it wasn't as though I was going to go off to do something terrible. I was going to volunteer. Could they really justify being mad about *that*?

When I got off the trolley car, I started to cross the street to go over to the animal shelter, but then I just stood there like an idiot. I hate the thought of lost and abandoned animals. *Any* stray animals. Did I really want to go in there? How likely *was* it that I wouldn't fall in love with every single dog and cat at the place, and want to bring them all home with me?

I got halfway up to the entrance and then turned around. I was going to have to think of something else to do. Something that didn't involve lost pets. I felt like a big failure, but it would be worse if I went in there and turned out to be a terrible volunteer.

I couldn't see an inbound trolley heading towards me, so I started walking. I could either get on the subway over on Huntington, or catch a bus back to Brighton, or Coolidge Corner. It was too cold just to stand around out here.

I was passing a large building complex on my right, but I didn't pay much attention to it, since I was too busy kicking myself for not having the nerve to go into the animal shelter. But then I looked again. It was a Veterans Administration Hospital. Veterans. From wars. I had known that there was one out here someplace, and that there was a Naval Hospital way on the other side of town in Chelsea — but I'd never given it much thought.

So, I went inside. It was a pretty big hospital — and hospitals really *do* give me the creeps — so it took me a while to find the right office. I ended up sitting across from a nice older lady named Mrs. Lipman, who worked for Patients' Services or something. I told her that I would like to volunteer, and she thought I meant just for today. She said that except for organizations like the Red Cross and the USO, volunteers usually only stopped by the VA Hospital on holidays and didn't come back again. Then she started asking me how old I was, what I had in mind, and if I had gotten permission from my parents.

I knew she was going to like some of my answers better than others, so I mainly stuck to the fact that I had been looking for a way to volunteer, that my brother was in Vietnam right now, and that this seemed like it might be the exact kind of thing I should be doing. She seemed to like the sound of that, although I could tell from her expression that she was assuming I would maybe show up once, and then lose interest. But after she talked to me for a while, she let me fill out some paperwork, and gave me other papers to bring home for my parents to sign.

I couldn't believe it when she told me there were patients in the hospital who had fought in *World War I*. I was wondering if they had been injured for decades, or if they had just gotten sick recently, but I was too shy to ask. But it was hard to imagine the idea of someone having been in the hospital nonstop since 1918. That was fifty years ago!

If you're offering to volunteer, I don't think it's right to have a lot of requirements about what you're willing to do, so I was glad that Mrs. Lipman seemed to understand that I was really hoping to be able to do something to help soldiers from Vietnam, specifically. She said that if I was sure I genuinely wanted to do this, they would be able to find plenty of things for me to do. But the next time I came back, I had to be sure and bring the papers signed by my parents — or, even better, bring one of my parents along.

She walked me out to the hall, and I was just starting to worry that maybe I was getting in a little over my head, when she called a nurse over.

"Do you have a minute, Lieutenant?" she asked.

The nurse paused only long enough to frown at us and say no.

But Mrs. Lipman motioned her over, anyway. The nurse looked kind of cranky, but she came back down the hallway. She was wearing a normal white uniform and cap, and the only difference was all of the military insignia. Her name tag said Dwyer, and she looked like she was about Brenda's age. Her hair was light brown and very short, and she was only about an inch taller than I am.

Mrs. Lipman explained who I was, and that I was a new volunteer who she thought might be a fine addition to the wards Lieutenant Dwyer supervised.

The nurse glanced at me briefly, said "I don't think so," and walked off.

But Mrs. Lipman wasn't having any of that. "Aren't you the same person who's been concerned about being so understaffed? Maybe Miss Flaherty will be able to help out."

The nurse frowned again. "How old is she?"

Had I left the corridor, and maybe not noticed myself doing it? "You know, ma'am, if you speak *really slowly*, my English is getting better and better every day," I said. I know that was rude, but I couldn't help it. She was being impolite, too.

At first Lieutenant Dwyer was obviously annoyed, but then I saw her look at me with slightly less suspicion. "Are you fluent yet?" she asked.

"I'm working on it, ma'am," I said. "Maybe in a year or two."

Mrs. Lipman seemed pleased by the way the conversation was going. She told us she would just let us get acquainted, made me promise not to come back without the signed papers, and said she hoped she'd see me again soon.

That left me, standing alone in the hallway, with a fairly hostile nurse. I was kind of intimidated — except that I've had Brenda pushing me around for years, so I'm used to it.

"Look, I'm sure you're a nice kid," Lieutenant Dwyer said. "But this really isn't going to be the right place for you. You have to appreciate the kind of patients we have here. They've been through so much, and —"

"My brother's at Khe Sanh," I said. "Out on Hill 881S."

Lieutenant Dwyer's eyebrows went up. Then she nodded a few times — to herself, I think — before looking at me. "Okay," she said. "We'll give it a try." Then she paused. "*One* try."

One try. Okay.

How come no one ever told me that volunteering was going to be this *complicated*?

February 13, 1968

I waited until tonight to tell my parents about the VA hospital, because when I got home yesterday afternoon, Dad had already left for work. It would probably have been easier to try and convince my mother first, but in case Dad was going to pitch a fit, I thought it would be better to wait until all three of us were together.

We watched the news, but they barely mentioned Khe Sanh, other than to say it was still under siege and several NVA divisions were expected to attack the base at any time. Which they tell us every day. Mom had already left the room, and Dad and I didn't say anything.

Then they showed some really shaky film of the fighting in Hue. The enemy has been occupying the city for the last couple of weeks, and the Marines are trying to drive them out.

After that, there was a long feature story about Senator Eugene McCarthy. There's a presidential election coming up in November, and he's trying to take the Democratic nomination away from President Johnson. He seems to be a good man, and his main political promise has been that he will end the war in Vietnam.

If I were old enough to vote, I would definitely be supporting him. Everyone in my family is a Democrat, but my father thinks that Senator McCarthy is too much of a "peacenik," so he's going to vote for President Johnson in the Massachusetts primary. I think we all wish that President Kennedy's brother, Senator Robert Kennedy, would run, but so far, he keeps saying no.

After we had been sitting at the dinner table for a while, my mother looked worried and asked me why I wasn't eating. I hadn't even noticed, because I was so busy thinking. I apologized and told her how delicious the stew was. As usual, the three of us weren't talking much. It's a lot easier when other people come over, because then we seem to be able to eat more normally.

At least tonight, I knew I had a conversation topic. I told them about volunteering, and they seemed really pleased about the idea — until they heard it was going to be at the VA hospital. So long, enthusiasm. My parents thought that sounded terrible, and were really quick to tell me all of the reasons why it was so terrible. I said okay, but that I'd already signed up, so it was too late.

Wouldn't it have been nice if that had worked?

After hearing "no," "absolutely not," and "you're

not allowed to do it" a few times, I lost my temper. It doesn't happen all that often, but when it does — *look out*. I ended up throwing my napkin and fork down, and storming away from the table. On top of which, I gave my bedroom door a *serious* slam when I got upstairs.

My father yelled for me to come right back down, I yelled that I wouldn't, and, well — it wasn't shaping up to be a very nice evening in the Flaherty house.

I patted Maggie and sulked for what felt like a really long time, but turned out to be only about twenty minutes. Then my mother knocked on the door and asked me to come back down to the table, please. I said no way. She said, "*Molly*," and — I went back downstairs.

My parents' plates had been cleared away, but mine was still there. I wanted to finish my dinner, because I was pretty hungry, but I pushed it away, instead. At first, no one spoke.

"Have you noticed that none of us really talk anymore?" I asked. "I mean, I can't stop worrying about him, either, but I feel like everyone's forgotten that *I'm* still here, you know? And it's hard to try and be good all the time, just so that no one will get upset. But shouldn't it matter when I get upset?"

I don't think my parents had expected this particular argument, and they looked guilty, especially since all three of us knew it was true. I also pointed out that I wasn't asking if I could go be a rock band groupie, or move into a crash pad in Central Square with my new pot-smoking friends, Amber and Rainbow, who I just met today on Boston Common; or if it would be okay for me to drop out of high school and go to Greenwich Village or Haight-Ashbury to try to "find myself." I was asking to do something that was, well, normal. Responsible. And maybe even worthwhile.

If Patrick had been here, he would have been whispering, "Oh, she has a silver tongue, an absolutely *silver* tongue." And then Dad would have gotten mad at him, which would have taken the heat off me, which would have been Patrick's motive in the first place.

I guess he would have gone away to college anyway this year, but it's *just so weird* not to have my backup here. No matter which one of us got in trouble, or why, we were always a team when it came to facing my parents, afterwards. Always.

My parents must have talked this over already, and made their decision, but my father was the one who spoke.

"We'd like to see you volunteer somewhere, but we just don't think that's the right environment for you," he said. "At least not until you're a little older. The place is going to be full of angry, young men, and —"

"What if we end up having an angry, young man living right here in the house?" I asked. "Will I have to move out?"

Now my father was stumped. He looked at my mother — and she seemed to be stumped, too.

"Would you drive me over the first day, Mom?" I asked. "So you can meet Mrs. Lipman, who's in charge?" Lieutenant Dwyer might not make as good an impression.

The room seemed more quiet than ever.

"Okay," my mother said finally.

February 17, 1968

Theresa and Laurel and I went downtown today to go to Filene's Basement and some of the other stores on Washington Street. Filene's is this huge, old department store, and the basement section has all of these great clothes, marked down to prices even we can afford sometimes. I get an allowance, and I do a little bit of babysitting for a few of our neighbors and Brenda's friends, but I won't be able to get a decent part-time job until this summer. Not too many places want to hire you until you're at least sixteen.

Every now and then Brenda offers to pay me for the babysitting I do at their house, but I always just pretend that I didn't hear her. For one thing, I know she and Hank don't have that much money, and for another, I like being around Jane and Gregory, so how could I get paid for that?

Theresa spends so much time practicing the piano, she would have trouble fitting a job into her schedule, and her parents don't want her to work during the school year, anyway. Laurel's uncle runs a pizza place, though, and he pays her to help take orders and bus tables for at least fifteen hours a week. So, among the three of us, she's the rich one. She's also, by far, the most interested in clothes, and always sees about ten things she wants in every single store. I like looking, and even trying things on — the more mod, the better, but when it comes to browsing, I get bored pretty quickly.

Except for bookstores, of course. I can spend hours in one of those, without even noticing that any time passed. I did end up buying some of the books about Vietnam that Mrs. Jorgensen recommended to me a couple of weeks ago.

After we finished wandering around the department stores — Laurel bought a paisley scarf, some bangle bracelets, and a bright orange headband — we went over to Bailey's to get ice-cream sundaes. I never mind spending money on ice cream.

Then we walked up to the Common for a while. It's the most famous old park in Boston (except maybe for *Fenway* Park, where the Red Sox play), and on warm days, there are people everywhere. Especially hippies. But it was pretty cold today, so I guess protesting the war and lounging around being groovy didn't seem quite as tempting as usual. And since it was Saturday, and there weren't any politicians around, there were only four or five people holding anti-war signs up in front of the State House.

We passed a group of black guys who were trying to look militant in berets and old fatigue jackets. Or maybe they actually *were* militant — it's sometimes hard to tell if people are really serious about making political statements, or if they just want everyone to think that they are. Anyway, some of them were laughing at us, and making cracks about rich, little white girls visiting from the suburbs.

That bugged me, since I'm not rich — and I'm not from the suburbs.

Theresa sighed. "Oh, great. Here we go."

"Don't let her do it," Laurel said, sounding really nervous. "They're going to get mad."

Some of the guys already looked mad, but the rest of them were still just laughing and making fun of us.

"Just so you know," I said to them. "We're not from the suburbs, we're *city*."

The ones who were laughing cracked up completely; a couple of the others scowled and clenched their fists.

"Ooh, baby," one of the younger ones said. "Here to tell us all about the ghet-to?"

My first instinct was to say, "Yeah, what do you want to know?" But I'm really trying to do a better job of not saying the first smart remark that pops into my head. So I said, "Nope. Just saying hello."

"Maybe you want to tell us you *dig* Dr. King, and

how you want to help us poor Negroes find a better life?" the same guy asked.

As a matter of fact, I *do* dig Dr. Martin Luther King. I think he's really brave, really smart — and completely cool. I hope I get to hear him give a speech in person someday.

"Why don't you run away now, little girl," one of the ones who wasn't laughing said. "Before we *chase* you."

One of the other guys stepped so close to me that I wanted to back up — but I didn't.

"I think you better go now," he said, very quietly.

I know he wanted to make me nervous, and I *was* a little nervous. But not as nervous as he probably wanted me to be. "Okay," I said, after a minute. "Nice talking to you. See you around."

I felt really self-conscious as I walked away, but I took my time. Some of the guys shouted stuff after me, which made me feel more sad than anything else.

"Make any new friends?" Theresa asked, her voice sounding really dry.

"No," I said. "Not even one." I hadn't really expected them to be friendly, but it's really awful to think that just saying hello to someone these days can start a big argument.

Sometimes, I think this country must be one of the most messed up places in the world.

February 19, 1968

Today was my first day to volunteer, and my mother drove me over to the VA hospital. I wasn't sure what I was supposed to wear, so I stayed in the plaid skirt and sweater I wore to school. My mother parked the car, but then didn't get out right away, so I was afraid she might have changed her mind about letting me do this.

"What?" I asked.

My mother shook her head. "I just think about my father sometimes, that's all."

My grandfather had died of a heart attack when I was four years old, so I don't remember him very well, but I know he fought in World War I. I'm not sure if there's a man anywhere on either side of the family who hasn't fought in a war.

I thought my mother was going to say something else, but she was already getting out of the car. Sometimes, I wonder what really goes on inside my mother's head. It must be hard to be so private, but I guess she likes it that way. I would ask her about it — but I don't think she'd tell me.

Mrs. Lipman seemed delighted to see me again, and she and my mother got along just fine. They talked for a while about the things I was going to be doing — like helping patients write letters home, while I just sat politely in my chair. Right before she left, my mother told me to call the firehouse when I was finished, so that my father could pick me up on his way home.

Then Mrs. Lipman took me upstairs, pointed out the ward where I was being assigned for today, and said, "Good luck!" There were a few guys in the hallway, wearing blue pajamas. They were either in wheelchairs or struggling along on crutches, while orderlies and a couple of nurses supervised them. Most of them didn't even look up when I walked by.

The orthopedics ward was more crowded — and much more noisy — than I'd expected. When I came in, everyone stopped what they were doing and stared at me. Then, some of the guys whistled and made catcalls, and for a second, I felt exactly the way I had in Boston Common the other day.

The room was long and narrow, and there was a row of about fifteen beds along each wall. There was a nurse's desk up at the front, with supply cabinets behind it. The patients looked even younger than I expected, and they were all wearing the same blue army pajamas I'd seen out in the hall. But they didn't really look military, because a lot of them also had on baseball caps or floppy green hats, and some of them even had on hippie stuff like love beads and thick leather bracelets.

But they were also missing arms or legs or — I'd never seen so many badly injured people in one place before, and it made me feel a little bit dizzy.

Lieutenant Dwyer was busy changing a boy's bandages, so she just nodded at me, instead of coming over.

"You look lost, sweetheart," someone said. "You sure you're in the right place?"

The voice was coming from a guy in a wheelchair who had rolled over next to me. He looked healthy, and athletic — but he was missing both legs below his knees. I know I wasn't supposed to flinch, but I did — and felt horrible for doing it. It just — surprised me, that's all. I knew they were all going to be hurt, but I hadn't expected — it was all really — I don't think I can describe it. I'll write more later.

Later —

No one in the hospital ward looked any older than my brother, and I suddenly hated the war twice as much as I ever had before.

Anyway, the guy in the wheelchair kept waving his hand in front of my face. "Hello," he said. "Did you go somewhere?"

I knew I had to pull myself together, since Lieutenant Dwyer probably wasn't coming over because she wanted to find out if I could handle all of this.

"Yeah," I said to the guy. "I have these . . . spells. It runs in my family."

The guy grinned. God, he was so young. If I saw him at school, I'm not sure I'd even think he was old enough to be a senior. "Well, we all got something wrong with us, right?" He put his hand out to shake mine. "I'm Jack. Thought you should know my name, in case we get married."

That made me relax. He just sounded like — a guy. A normal, regular guy. One of my brother's friends. "I'm Molly," I said. "I'm already engaged — but we can talk about it."

Jack spun his wheelchair around. "This is Molly," he

said to the ward in general. "And I just want all of you to know that I saw her first."

That got a lot of comments, and some of the other guys started throwing stuff at him. I automatically caught an empty Coke can that was coming right towards me and flipped it back — which got a big laugh.

Lieutenant Dwyer — who had been watching all of this like a hawk — came over now. "Guys, this is Molly," she said, and paused. "What's your last name again?"

"Flaherty," I said.

She nodded. "Right." She turned her attention back to the ward. "This is Molly Flaherty, and she's going to be volunteering here today. So, try not to scare her off."

A guy in one of the beds behind me raised the stump that had once been his left arm. "This scare you?" he asked, and I could hear the edge in his voice.

"Nope," I said.

"Watch it, Cowboy," Jack said from his wheelchair. "That's my fiancée you're talking to."

"You *wish,* man," said a guy who was lying in bed, his lower body so still that he must have been paralyzed.

"She's deeply in love with me, Vince," Jack said. "You gotta trust me on this one."

While they were all joking around, Lieutenant

Dwyer brought over a stack of fresh linens. "You any good at changing sheets?"

I assumed she wanted the truth. "I'm a little sloppy," I said.

She shrugged and handed me the pile. "You'll learn." She pointed to some empty beds further down the ward. "Those four need to be done before the guys get back from physical therapy."

I looked down at Jack. "Think she wants me to salute?"

"You better, yeah," he said.

Lieutenant Dwyer just shook her head, and I decided to be smart and go change the sheets.

I know I've only been there once so far, but I have a feeling that this volunteering just might work out.

February 23, 1968

Letters from Patrick are coming almost every day lately, but he says he hasn't been getting any of ours for a few weeks. That must mean that a lot of those care packages my mother keeps patiently packing up have gotten lost, too. Apparently the helicopters just drop their loads of food and mail and everything, instead of landing on the hill, because Patrick says the NVA shoots them down, otherwise. But if the wind's blowing, or the helicopter pilot doesn't have very good aim, a lot of supplies end up landing in the wrong place. If they roll down the hill, outside the base perimeter, then they have to be destroyed, so that the enemy won't be able to take any of the stuff. So Patrick's convinced that most of his mail is getting blown up on a regular basis. He says they're always a lot more upset about that, than they are about losing the deliveries of food and water and ammunition.

Last week, he sent two letters addressed to me, at our house, so they were ones I knew he didn't mind having my parents read, too. All the first one said was, "You may skip early Mass, but please say four Hail Marys."

Well, *I* thought it was funny.

The other one was full of questions about what's been going on at school, how all the teams are doing, and that kind of thing. He finished it by asking if I could subtly find out Audrey Taylor's address at college — which I'm pretty sure was the main reason he wrote the letter at all. I don't know if calling her mother was subtle, but it seemed like the easiest way to do it. I hope he does write to her — I think they would be really cute together. And when I saw her at Betsy's New Year's Eve party, I definitely got the feeling that she wouldn't mind hearing from him. While I was at it, I called Mrs. Finnegan and asked her for Eddie's address in Vietnam. I'd like to know how he's doing over there. Mrs. Finnegan told me that he's more than halfway through his tour now, and they're just counting the days until he can come home.

Khe Sanh is still the major news story coming out of Vietnam. They never seem to say anything about the hills, but when they show news films taken at the main base, the reporters are always wearing helmets and flak jackets, and they keep ducking as explosions go off someplace behind them. It looks really bad.

The photographs and articles in *Life* and *Newsweek* make the situation seem even worse. You can count on there being at least one shot of a wounded Marine with a cigarette hanging out of his mouth. They always look tough, and tired — and haunted. They also show pictures of Marines running for cover during mortar attacks. But the photographs of dead bodies are the worst of all. Why do they even print those? American *or* Vietnamese. It seems so — disrespectful.

Usually, most of the articles include really detailed maps, and I hate seeing Patrick's hill out there all by itself, a few miles away from the main base. The reporters who write the articles keep describing the hills as being "the end of the line" for Khe Sanh. The last defense. And since 881S is the furthest one out, I guess Patrick's hill is the *real* end of the line. It must be so scary for him.

My grandmother came over for supper tonight, and in spite of everything, we all had a nice time. She and my mother definitely do some bickering, but lately, my mother also seems a lot more cheerful when she's around. So Gram comes over from Medford more often than usual.

After we finished eating, they stayed in the kitchen, drinking tea and talking, while my father and I went into the living room. I had noticed that my parents were making a point of spending more time with me lately.

He and I decided to watch the Celtics game, while we waited for a *Perry Mason* rerun to come on. We both really like that show, and sometimes I think I might want to be a lawyer, instead of a veterinarian. But then again, we also like *Ironside,* and I'm sure I *don't* want to be a police detective.

Pretty sure, anyway.

A stack of Patrick's latest letters was on the coffee table, and Dad started reading the one on the top. I think it was the one where he kept writing about how tired he was, but didn't say much more than that. So, it was clear that bad things were happening — and he just wasn't telling us. There was something I'd been wondering about, and this seemed like a reasonable time to bring it up.

"There are a lot of friends he doesn't seem to mention anymore," I said.

My father nodded, so I guess he had noticed it, too.

"Does that mean what I think it does?" I asked.

My father hesitated, but then he nodded again.

Damn.

Poor Patrick.

Today was my second time at the VA hospital.

"Hey, Lieutenant!" Jack said, when I walked into the ward. "You owe me five dollars!" He pointed at a guy in bed whose legs were both in traction. "You, too, Morgenthal. Pay up!"

Lieutenant Dwyer looked faintly surprised to see me — most of the guys did, too, for that matter — but she put me right to work changing sheets and passing out cups of orange juice.

I was much less nervous today, so I spent more time looking around and trying to get a feel for the place. The main thing, of course, is how badly injured all of them are. Since this is an orthopedics ward, that means that most of the injuries involve bones and muscles. All thirty beds are full right now — and apparently, they always are, because if someone gets well enough to go home, another soldier arrives right away to take his place. Sometimes, it gets so crowded here that patients end up sleeping on gurneys out in the halls.

I'd say that at least twenty of these guys are dealing with amputations. An arm, a leg, a hand, a foot — or, in some cases, more than one amputation. There are

121

three boys who are paralyzed from the waist down, and a couple of others whose faces are almost completely bandaged — I'm not sure why. There are also a few in different kinds of body casts, who either broke a lot of bones all at once, or else fractured really major bones, which take a really long time to heal.

Some of the guys, like Jack, are amazingly cheerful and funny, but there are others who don't speak at all. In fact, they don't even look at me. Lieutenant Dwyer told me that most of the them almost never get any visitors. Sometimes it's because they're originally from someplace hundreds of miles away. I thought all of the patients would be from the Boston area, or southern New England, anyway, but the Army's only requirement for sending them here is that they have to be from a state east of the Mississippi River. I assume they try to place guys as close to their homes as possible, but it also depends upon which hospital has enough room, or if the soldier has a specific kind of injury — like burns, or vision problems. Then, he might get sent to a hospital that specializes in treating that particular thing.

But the other reason that some of these guys don't get visitors, is because their families or girlfriends don't want to see them anymore, now that they've been maimed. I couldn't even believe that, but Lieutenant Dwyer says it happens all the time, especially with girlfriends. Sometimes they will even show up to see the guy, take one look — and leave. I still couldn't quite imagine that, but Jack and his good friend Vincent — who's paralyzed from the mid-chest down — both said, "Oh, yeah, it happens a lot."

That definitely explains why so many of the guys look so depressed. To be injured *and* abandoned?

That stinks.

February 27, 1968

The newscasters usually don't give their opinions about anything, but tonight, for once, Walter Cronkite broke that rule. He sat there, behind his desk, and told everyone watching that things had gotten so bad in Vietnam that he didn't think we could win the war, and that he doesn't think we should be over there. Apparently, he had gone there to see it for himself. And if there's any public figure I'd trust to tell us the truth, it's

Walter Cronkite. I don't feel that way about politicians anymore.

Since President Johnson doesn't seem to listen to what ordinary people think, I wonder if he'll pay attention this time?

And if he doesn't, I hope that Senator McCarthy beats him in the primaries. Hey, at this point, I'd rather see Richard Nixon be President.

Almost anything would be better than the way things are right now.

February 28, 1968

Today was Ash Wednesday, and naturally, my whole family went to church. I never know what to give up for Lent, but we're supposed to make some sort of personal sacrifice during the forty days until Easter. When I was little, I would just give up ice cream, or candy. It wasn't even that hard, because my mother didn't let me eat much of that stuff, anyway.

"You could give up television," Brenda suggested, at supper tonight. She and Hank had brought the kids over about an hour earlier.

"God's compassionate, remember?" I said. "He's only supposed to ask what we can deliver."

Hank's contribution was, "Molly, you're a very sad case — don't ever let them tell you different."

Maybe so.

But I know one thing for sure. If someone told me that my not watching television would guarantee that Patrick would get home safe and sound — I'd never turn it on again.

March 1, 1968

I haven't been telling many people about volunteering, but the word seems to be getting around, anyway. Anything that relates to Vietnam gets all sorts of reactions, and this isn't any different. "Oh, cool" and "Yeah. So?" are the two most common. I've also been called a war lover, and "as bad as the soldiers themselves." A couple of people have asked if they can volunteer, too, and I told them they just had to go over to the hospital and sign up if they wanted. Both of them looked as though that sounded like too much work, so I don't think I'll hold my breath. And — I hate to admit it — but I'm a real jerk, because my first thought was, hey, this was my idea first, go find your own volunteer job. I didn't say it or anything, but I thought it. It's not like I own the idea of volunteering at a VA hospital — lots of people do it, all over the country — but it bugs me when you do something, and people immediately want to turn around and copy you.

How immature is that? Pretty immature.

During gym class, Karen and Ursula asked me if going over to the VA hospital was a good way to meet cute guys.

No, I'm not even going to write it down — I'll just *think* it.

March 3, 1968

I actually had a good time yesterday. (I feel like it's been months since I've said that — or felt it.) Laurel had to work, so she couldn't come, but Theresa and Dorothy and I decided that it was going to be Movie Day. We went to see *The Jungle Book* and *The Producers,* and both of them were great.

Then we spent the night at Theresa's house, eating her mother's lasagna and watching silly shows like *Get Smart* and *Petticoat Junction*. We even spent a couple of hours trying — and failing — to make some decent-looking tie-dyed shirts. They all came out this same sort of muddy brown color, but it was still really funny trying to do it. Maybe I'll wear mine sometimes, when I'm safely inside the house, where no one I know would have any chance of seeing me, including my own family.

I really have to remember to have fun a little more often.

March 4, 1968

Today was my VA day. I'm finding that you can tell how things are going that day within about thirty seconds of walking onto the ward. Almost all of the guys spend a lot of time at physical therapy every day, and when they get back upstairs, they're usually very tired and in a lot of pain. Sometimes, they're scheduled to have surgery of various kinds, and on those days, they come back all groggy and usually feeling sick to their stomachs.

Whatever mood floats around the ward becomes really contagious. So, if one guy is really happy, because he just heard from his girlfriend or found out that he was going to be allowed to go home soon, the entire ward seems cheerful. At the same time, if any of the guys get bad news, the whole place plunges into depression.

Since I can't help do anything medical, I figure my main job is to try and read the mood of the day — and brighten it, if possible. I'm starting to learn more people's names, and get a sense of what they're like. Everyone on the ward is in the Army — the Marines and sailors are over at the Naval Hospital in Chelsea, and I'm not sure where the Air Force sends their wounded soldiers. They were all injured in Vietnam, except for one poor kid who had both legs crushed when he slipped and fell during a routine training exercise at Fort Devens. Apparently, he got run over by an Army truck, and they don't think he'll ever walk again.

I had assumed that all of the Vietnam guys would have been injured in combat, but quite a few were working in base camps, and got hurt during rocket attacks and things like that. Last week, Jack told me that

Nelson, in Bed 25, lost his hands — and probably his vision; they aren't sure yet — when he and a buddy were goofing around inside their tent at Cu Chi, and a grenade hanging from his friend's web gear went off by accident. Nelson's friend was killed instantly.

Today's mood was pretty low, because one of the guys who lost his leg took a bad fall at PT this morning. He landed so hard that he got a slight concussion and broke his elbow. That spooked everyone else, especially the guys who are also trying to learn how to walk on new prostheses. I felt stupid bringing around cups of juice, so that Lieutenant Dwyer could hand out the different medications everyone was supposed to take, because so many of the guys were in lousy moods and would barely look at me. Two of them even knocked the cups over — purposely, I think — when I set them down on their rickety little bedside tables. But, I just went to get a towel, cleaned the messes up, and brought them fresh cups.

I was tempted to pretend to have a headache, and ask Lieutenant Dwyer if I could go home early. But she was really distracted, because one of the guys who had had surgery earlier was groaning from the pain and running a fever — and she was also covering the ward directly across the hall. So I knew I shouldn't bother her.

Even Jack was subdued today, and he was lying in bed, instead of cruising around in his wheelchair. His friend Vincent was either asleep — or pretending to be.

An orderly whose name I didn't know was mopping the floor, starting from the back of the ward, and either he was in a bad mood, too, or he was really clumsy, because he kept bumping into things. A couple of times, he jarred people's beds by accident, and the guy lying there would groan and swear at him.

Lieutenant Dwyer was in and out, because of whatever she was doing over in the other ward, and the next time she left, I went over and sat down behind her desk.

"Okay, people," I said loudly. "New rules, starting now. I don't want to see any talking. I don't want to see any smiles. I don't want to see any fun. All I want to see is *healing,* got it? Lots and lots of healing."

Well, the one thing I had gotten was almost everyone's full attention. Some guys were staring, some guys were frowning, and some of them were starting to smile.

"Well, *heal,*" I said, doing a pretty fair imitation of my father's bark. "Now!"

Tiger, a double amputee in Bed 6, laughed, but it sounded more than a little bitter. "Yeah. Easy for you to say."

I turned to look at him. "Is that talking I hear, son? I don't *like* talking. And, you know what else I don't like?" I took a clean pillowcase from the cabinet and tied a few knots in it until it — sort of — resembled a lumpy cloth football. Then I tossed it to him and he caught it with his remaining hand. "I don't like people who throw things around and make my ward disorderly."

"Hey, over here, man!" Jack said to Tiger.

Tiger threw him the pillowcase, and Jack passed it to Vincent, who passed it down to Jose in Bed 20, who had lost his right foot. I tied another pillowcase into the same shape, and threw it into the ward, too.

"You know what else I don't like?" I said, as half the ward threw the pillowcases around. Norman, who was paralyzed from the waist down, flipped one to me, and I sent it sailing down towards Bed 15, where a guy named Bruce caught it, and passed it on. "I don't like it when *everyone* who has a radio turns it on *really loud,* at the exact same time."

Immediately, transistor radios all over the ward

began snapping on. A lot of them were tuned to different stations, so the noise definitely fell into the loud category. Lieutenant Dwyer must have heard it from across the hall, because she hurried back in.

"What's going on here?" she asked, looking perplexed — and irritated.

There was a definite pause in the chaos, while most of the guys waited to hear how I was going to answer her.

"Spring training," I said. "We're doing routine infield drills. Trying to get ready for Opening Day."

"Oh," she said, and looked around. I would have expected her to get mad, but maybe she was just glad to see that the general mood had changed. "Well, can you do them a little more quietly?"

I nodded. "Absolutely. But we *do* have to keep throwing and kicking the balls around."

She waited until some of the guys had turned their radios down, and then she nodded, too. "Okay, then," she said. "Play ball."

So, we played ball.

March 9, 1968

Today, I turned sixteen. Finally! Now I can get my driver's license and everything.

Theresa and Laurel both came over for supper, along with my grandmother, Brenda, and my niece and nephew. My father had gotten another captain to cover part of his tour, so that he could come home for a couple of hours and be at the party.

I got a lot of great gifts. A bunch of books — mostly novels, a new sweater, a blue striped shirt, socks, some records, and — best of all — a typewriter! My father kept apologizing because it's secondhand, but I think it's *great*.

And since my handwriting is so awful, I bet my teachers are going to think so, too.

In fact, they maybe even chipped in to help him pay for it.

We had gotten a letter from Patrick a few days ago that said, "Do Not Open Until March 9th. This means *you,* kid." He had made a birthday card by folding a piece of USO stationery in half and covered the front with little flowers and stars — and an amazingly good drawing of Maggie. Then I saw a little note scribbled at the bottom: *"My friend Rotgut did this. Not bad, huh?"* Not bad at all. In fact, it was really good.

Inside, the card said, *"Happy Birthday, Molly! Please be kind to the Studebaker. I'm sorry I couldn't send you a gift, but now I owe you an extra-good one, right? Love, from your very favorite brother, Patrick."*

My only brother, but yes, also my favorite.

Best of all, he had enclosed a photograph — the first one we had seen of him since he left. It showed him posing with three other guys in front of a bunker. One of them was a lean black kid with a great smile, one was a pudgy white kid who was squinting, and the third guy was just standing there looking serious and holding an M-16. Patrick himself looked great. He was pretty muddy, and he'd maybe lost a little weight, but he was grinning his same old Patrick grin, and wearing the Red Sox cap we'd mailed him. On the back of the picture, it said: *"This is one of our bunkers here on the hill. All the comforts of home — except for the actual comfort of home. Oh, well. Happy birthday! The guys in the picture are my best buddy Bebop, Pugsley, and Perez. I'm the one on the left. But you knew that. Right? Love, Patrick."*

We all spent a lot of time passing the picture around because it was so great to actually be able to *see* Patrick, and how he looked. I wonder if he realized how great a present it was going to be — for all of us?

It certainly made *my* day.

Later —

It really was a swell birthday. We had some of my favorite foods for supper — chicken, rice pilaf, carrots, chocolate cake. And hey, I even got to watch *Mannix* after everyone went home!

The show was just ending when my mother came downstairs, holding a small package wrapped in white tissue paper. I was surprised, since I'd already gotten so many other presents today. It was obviously a book of some kind, which wasn't a big surprise.

"Thank you," I said, when she handed it to me. "Did you forget to give it to me before?"

My mother actually turned a little bit red. "No, I just thought I'd give it to you when we were alone," she said.

That made me a little uneasy, since that meant it was probably going to be a book explaining sex. Okay, maybe I've only kissed a couple of boys before, but I still think I have a pretty good handle on it. It mean, I'm *sixteen*.

"You know, I saw a film at school, Mom," I said. "It covered ovulation, and everything."

My mother just motioned for me to open it. The paperback was called *The Feminine Mystique* by a person named Betty Friedan. I had heard of it before, but I didn't really know what it was about.

"Thank you," I said. "Is it about how beautiful it is to grow into a woman?" I've only gotten my period three times so far, starting last fall — but that still counts, right? I was the last one of my friends to get it, which made me feel pretty stupid. At least I'm younger than most of them, which makes it slightly less embarrassing to be behind everyone else. But only slightly.

My mother had a funny expression on her face. Distant, kind of. "No," she said. "Not exactly."

So now I was curious, and I asked her if she'd given it to Brenda, too.

"She didn't really like it," my mother said.

Brenda doesn't read much, anyway — she thinks it's boring, except for news magazines, and maybe Agatha Christie. And she also goes through *The Boston Globe* and *The Record American* page by page, every single day, so I guess she'd mostly rather just read about current events.

"It's — political," my mother said.

Cool!

March 10, 1968

At church today, we found out that Eddie Finnegan got wounded a couple of days ago, and he's on his way home. Mr. Finnegan looked very tense, and Mrs. Finnegan was crying, both because she's worried — and because she's so relieved. All she really knows is that he got shot in the leg, and it will take him a while to get better, but he should be just fine. At least, that's what the Army is telling them.

Thank God for that.

In the car on the way home, my parents and I were pretty quiet.

"Well, let's just be glad that their son is on his way home," my father said.

"Amen to that," my mother said, and I nodded.

Apparently, all three of us had been thinking the exact same wistful thing.

March 12, 1968

The New Hampshire primary was today, and Senator McCarthy got forty-two percent of the vote. All of the polls had been predicting that President Johnson would come away with a huge margin of victory, and now it looks as though Senator McCarthy is a serious candidate, after all. President Johnson hasn't been spending that much time campaigning, but if he wants to win the nomination, he's definitely going to have to start trying a little harder.

Richard Nixon is the front-runner in the Republican party, and he got *seventy-eight percent* of the votes in the primary. So, unless the other candidates, George Romney and Nelson Rockefeller, do some serious catching up, it looks like Nixon will win his nomination easily.

I'm not sure I like *any* of the candidates, in either party, but if I had to pick one, it would definitely be Senator McCarthy.

Anyway, something weird — and a little creepy — happened earlier today. I got a letter from Eddie Finnegan, dated about ten days ago, before he got wounded. It was a nice note, saying that it was great to hear from me, and he was really homesick. He said he was stationed near Chu Lai, with the 196th Light Infantry Brigade, and that while Vietnam was a lousy place, there were some great guys in his platoon. He also asked how Patrick was doing, and if it was true that he was up at Khe Sanh. Although he didn't come right out and say so, I could tell that he was having a really tough time, especially since he didn't even mention the Red Sox once. Eddie has to be the biggest fan I've ever met — and I've met some *world-class* Red Sox fans.

It's just really disturbing to think of that letter traveling innocently through the mail — while in the meantime, its author ended up lying in an evacuation hospital somewhere with a bullet in his leg.

If the same thing ever happened with one of Patrick's letters — but I'm not going to think about that. All I'm going to tell myself is that he's fine. Perfectly fine.

And that he's going to stay that way.

March 17, 1968

Senator Robert Kennedy held a news conference yesterday and announced that he's going to run for

President, after all. Now *that* is a good St. Patrick's Day present. The announcement was carried live, here in Boston, and when he finished speaking, I actually heard cheers coming from some of the other houses in the neighborhood.

Not only do I like him, but I also think he can beat Richard Nixon in November. On top of that, I think he'll make an *excellent* President. In his speech, he said his main goals were to help reunify the country after so many years of tension and turmoil — and to end the war in Vietnam.

I think he's going to be the best thing to happen to America since — well, since his brother was the President.

I bet Senator McCarthy's disappointed, though. He wasn't even the front-runner for a full week.

After mass this morning, Mrs. Finnegan told my mother that Eddie's been transferred out of Vietnam, to an army hospital in Japan. And then, in a couple of weeks, he's going to be sent to the army hospital at Fort Dix, New Jersey, to recuperate. It would have been so nice if he'd been assigned to the VA here in Boston — but I guess the Army had other ideas.

As far as I can tell, the Army usually has other ideas.

And considering that the USMC is making the Marines sit at Khe Sanh, week after week, waiting to see if the NVA is going to get the nerve to mount an attack, it seems like they have some pretty dumb ideas, too.

It's like that old joke — which I've heard about ten times at the VA hospital.

Military intelligence? *No such thing.*

March 20, 1968

I've been reading the book my mother gave me for my birthday, and it's not at all what I expected it to be. It's all about women's rights, and whether the concept of "The Happy Housewife" is a myth. The author feels that women have spent too many years doing all the drudge work, without being given the same opportunities to work outside the home that men have. I agree with that completely — and I guess my mother does, too, or she wouldn't have given me the book. But I can't help worrying that maybe she regrets the fact that she got married and had children. Had us.

So, I asked her tonight, while my father was downstairs watching the Celtics game. She said that she wasn't sorry about the choices she had made, but that she thought women ought to have *more* choices. The same choices men have. She also said that she hoped I would be able to explore some of the different opportunities that she had skipped.

"Does Dad know you feel this way?" I asked.

She grinned suddenly, in the sort of quick, flashing way that I associate with Patrick, and it made her look at least ten years younger.

"I think he's beginning to suspect," she said.

Hmm. From the sounds of it, that could get interesting.

March 22, 1968

I wasn't too excited about the idea, but Theresa talked me into showing up at the big Spring Dance at school tonight. She's going with a senior named Tom, who plays first trumpet in the band. They aren't quite officially going steady, but she really likes him — and it seems to be mutual. I was afraid I would be the only one there without a date, but the guy Laurel was going with came down with strep throat, and Dorothy Chamberlin doesn't have a date, either.

The dance was semi-formal, which meant that we wore dresses instead of skirts, and the boys wore ties, instead of open collars. Other than that, it was like every other school dance I'd ever gone to, with incompetent amateur disk jockeys, and limp crepe paper decorations trying to disguise the fact that we were actually just in the gymnasium.

I'm not very good at dancing — even though I must have seen *American Bandstand* a hundred times over the years. But watching other people dance doesn't seem to be a very good learning technique. For me, anyway.

But I danced with five different guys from the football team, and each of them asked about Patrick, and seemed genuinely interested in hearing the answers. I just wish I had more answers.

I went out to the hallway to get a drink of water at one point, and when I walked back in, I seemed to be the only person in the entire gym who wasn't dancing with someone. I felt really uncomfortable, standing by the bleachers all by myself, and I was about to go back out to the hall, when — of all people — *Jason* came over. He was wearing gray flannel slacks, with a white

Oxford shirt and a skinny black tie — and yes, he looked cute. Very cute. I might not like him anymore, but I still think he's attractive.

"Um, hi," he said. Well, no — he *mumbled*.

I said hi back, and we stood there, while everyone else danced to a song by the Temptations.

"You look nice," he said.

I thanked him, and told him he did, too. And we stood there. Were he and Cathy Watkins still going out? I didn't even know. It had been a long time since I'd noticed, one way or the other.

He cleared his throat, shifted his weight, and then cleared his throat again. "So — you want to dance?"

The minute I start thinking that I understand boys, I realize all over again that I don't have a clue.

"Sure, Jason," I said. "Why not?"

March 25, 1968

Today, I spent almost the entire afternoon playing poker. It wasn't exactly what I had in mind, when I decided to volunteer — but, hey, it was fun. When I got to the ward, there was already a rowdy game going on, with people gathered around Sam Morgenthal's bed. Because he's in traction, he can't move, so I guess they decided to bring the game to him.

"Hey, Molly!" Vincent said cheerfully. "You going to play?"

I looked over at Lieutenant Dwyer, who was already taking out a stack of fresh linens from the supply closet.

"Not yet," I said to Vincent. "But save a place for me."

There were seven guys playing, plus five more down at physical therapy, so I had about a dozen beds to change. But, practice makes perfect, right? I also emptied all of the wastebaskets, straightened up people's bedside tables, and cleared away all of the empty juice and water glasses.

Then I was ready to play.

Except for one little detail — I didn't know how.

The guys seemed to think that was just about the funniest thing they had ever heard, and they took turns giving me complicated — and confusing — instructions. It's a good thing that they were only playing for pennies, or I think I would have backed out.

I lost the first five hands in a row, and Vincent won three of them.

"How come he keeps winning?" I asked Jack.

Jack shrugged, checking his latest hand. "Because he cheats."

I looked over at Vincent, slouching in his wheelchair. "Do you cheat?"

"Oh, yeah," he said, without a trace of guilt. "All the time."

I looked around at everyone else. "Does it bother you guys?"

"No, not really," Cowboy said, flipping through his cards one-handed — since he only *had* one hand.

"How come?" I asked.

He shrugged. "Because all of us cheat, too."

I saw the rest of them nodding.

Oh. No *wonder* I kept losing.

I played for a while — losing every single time — and then went over to Lieutenant Dwyer to see if there was anything else she wanted me to do. She thought that over, and then indicated Bed 10. I'd never heard the guy lying there say a word, and he always seemed to be in the exact same position, every time I came, as if he never moved at all from week to week. His face was heavily bandaged, and he was one of the ones who was probably going to be almost completely blind — as well as crippled, since he'd lost his right leg, too. The only two things I knew about him were that his name was Ray, and he was very depressed.

Well, I could try. I walked over there.

"Hi, Ray, I'm Molly," I said.

He didn't respond.

"You need anything?" I asked.

He didn't respond.

"Well, those guys are wiping me out at poker, so I think I'll stay over here for a while," I said.

Still no response. So I just sat there, and chattered away about school, about the Red Sox, about anything that came into my head. Other than breathing, he never seemed to move. After about half an hour, I was ready to give up, but I thought I'd make one more attempt.

"So, were you in I Corps?" I asked. "My brother is in I Corps."

He didn't say anything, but he maybe — just slightly — turned his head. And I realized that other people on the ward were listening, too, since I don't think I'd mentioned Patrick to them before. So, I told Ray about how he was a really great football player, but he'd joined the Marines, ended up at Khe Sanh — the whole story. Or, as Patrick would say, the whole nine yards.

"So, that's why you come here?" Ray asked. "Pity?"

Hey, wait. Was that a *voice*? I glanced over at Lieutenant Dwyer, who smiled. So I must have been on the right track.

"No," I said. "Just looking for a hobby."

Ray made some kind of sound. It wasn't a laugh — but he wasn't telling me to go away, either.

"So, are we going to have a conversation?" I asked him.

He shook his head.

"Think we will next time?" I asked.

He shook his head.

"Did I just waste a good chunk of my afternoon?" I asked.

"Hey, it's *your* damn hobby," he said.

So it was.

March 27, 1968

I got my driver's license today!

Enough said.

March 31, 1968

My father was involved with a five-alarm fire at a church in the Back Bay night before last, and he's still tired. So I'm really glad that he had today off. Miraculously, no one was seriously injured, but the fire spread to about twelve other buildings, and the jakes had a tough fight knocking it down. Dad's company was heavily involved with the interior attack — which means that they were leading the way and using their hoses to hit what they call "the seat of the fire" directly.

Hank took in a lot of smoke, and he had to spend Friday night and most of Saturday at Mass General Hospital. He seems to be fine now, but it definitely gave all of us a scare. One of Dad's other men fell and wrenched his back pretty badly, so he'll be out of commission for a while, and Ramirez, from the ladder company, broke his ankle when the roof he was on caved in partway. I don't think people always realize how dangerous it is to be a firefighter. This particular fire started off as a fairly routine job in an empty church — and turned into a huge five-alarmer within the space of a few minutes.

Then again, Dad says that there's no such thing as a

routine fire. I'm just glad that he's okay — and that Hank is, too.

President Johnson appeared on television tonight, live. I assumed he was going to give a speech about the Presidential primaries — or maybe even about what's happening at Khe Sanh, but it didn't work out that way. Whenever the President — any President — addresses the nation during prime time, you always have to assume that he has something important to say. Otherwise, it wouldn't interrupt regularly scheduled programming, right?

So my parents and I sat in the living room, and waited to hear what he was going to say. I know *I* was hoping that he was going to announce that he was either pulling the Marines out of Khe Sanh — or sending thousands of other Marines in there to help.

Instead, he looked into the camera very seriously, and told the country that he was ordering a complete bombing halt over North Vietnam, with the hope that the enemy would then be willing to sit down and discuss a possible peace negotiation. That was big news, all by itself, but then he said that the Vietnam War had to be his top priority, and he didn't want to waste any of his energy doing less important things. So, he said that he "shall not seek and will not accept the nomination of his party for the Presidency of the United States." Or something like that. In other words, despite everything we've been hearing for months, President Johnson is *not* going to run for reelection. It was the last thing any of us had expected him to say, and the commentators who came on afterwards seemed just as stunned by the announcement.

Wow. I wasn't quite sure what to think, so I looked at my parents.

"Is this good news or bad news?" I asked.

"Well — it's good news for Senator Kennedy," my father said.

It's *great* news for Senator Kennedy.

April 1, 1968

When I got to the VA today, all of the guys were still talking about President Johnson's speech last night. None of them seemed to believe that North Vietnam would be willing to negotiate, and most of them thought that the bombing halt was only going to endanger American troops who normally depended upon that extra protection to keep the NVA from infiltrating into South Vietnam.

But they all seemed happy to hear that President Johnson had dropped out of the Presidential race. Or, as Jack put it, "Hey, if he hadn't started this stupid war, I'd still be able to wear shoes."

I don't think anyone could put it more clearly than *that*.

April 4, 1968

Today was just terrible. I can't believe it, but Dr. Martin Luther King is dead. He was assassinated in Memphis, Tennessee. By a white man.

Dr. King was a man who preached peace, and unity, and hope — and because of that, someone killed him.

My God, I think America really *has* gone crazy.

April 6, 1968

My father came home tonight for the first time in three days. Once the news broke that Dr. King had been assassinated, rioting began in black neighborhoods all over the city. On television, I heard that there have been riots in more than 125 cities across the country. And one thing that goes along with riots, is lots and lots of fires. My father had been checking in with my mother every few hours since Thursday, but each time he thought it might be safe to leave the firehouse, another series of calls would come in, and off they'd go.

When he walked in, the first thing we saw was the white bandage taped to his forehead.

My mother jumped up from her chair. "What happened, Sean? Are you all right?"

He nodded, gave us each a hug, and then sat down heavily at the kitchen table. My mother got him a beer, and he said thank you, but he seemed to be too tired to lift up the glass.

My mother sat across from him, clasping her hands tightly together the way she does when she's trying to stay calm. "Are things any better out there?" she asked, her voice more calm than I would have predicted.

My father yawned, and nodded. "Yeah. I think the rioters got tired, too. You can only loot and pillage for so long, you know?"

I felt better when he said that, because if he could

make a joke, then he must be okay. But I still asked him what happened to his head, and my mother leaned forward, waiting to hear the answer, too.

My father slowly picked up his glass and took a large sip. "They set a row of cars on fire, and when we got there, no one in the neighborhood was happy to see us."

"*And,*" my mother said impatiently.

"I'm fine," he said. "I got hit with a bottle, that's all. Or maybe it was a rock. I'm not sure." Then he smiled at her. "I'm *fine,* Colleen. Really."

I can understand why the black community is heartbroken and angry about what happened to Dr. King. We all are. But, why would anyone throw rocks and bottles at *firefighters,* who were just trying to help? That doesn't make any sense to me at all.

"So then what?" I asked.

My father shrugged. "Pulled my men out until we could get a police escort in there."

I thought about that. "And then, you went back?"

"Of course we did," my father said. "There was a *fire.*"

Right.

I might be wrong, but I think Dr. King would be horrified if he knew that this was the way so many of his followers had reacted to his death. If you ask me, it's an insult to his memory — and to everything he believed in.

It's probably just as well that no one has asked me.

April 8, 1968

I was sitting in trigonometry this afternoon, when a message came from the office for me to go and call my mother right away. I was so sure that it was going to be bad news — about Patrick or my father, or someone else in the family — that I pretty much ran down to the alcove where the school pay phones are. By the time I got there, I felt as though I couldn't quite get my breath, and I had to take a few seconds to try and calm down. My hands were shaking, so I had a little bit of trouble dialing.

"Don't worry," my mother said, once she had answered the phone. "It's good news."

I sank back against the wall of the phone booth, so relieved that I wasn't sure I could speak.

"The Army and some South Vietnamese soldiers got to Khe Sanh today, and they're taking over the base," my mother said. "I just saw it on the news. The siege is over."

It was over? Just like that? Now I *really* wanted to sit down.

It was over. Patrick was safe. For now, anyway.

Wow!

It was Monday, so it was my day to go over to the VA hospital. I couldn't wait to tell all of the guys, since they might not have heard the news yet. Maybe they didn't know Patrick personally — but I knew they would be almost as happy about it as I am. Especially Jack and Vincent — and maybe even Ray.

But when I stepped into the ward, I knew that something was very wrong. I wasn't sure what it was, but I had never felt such a dark silence in there before. I had been about to say, "Hey! Guess what?" but I managed to stop myself just in time.

No one was talking, and they were all staring into space, or lying down with their arms — if they still had arms — covering their faces.

"Hi," I said uncertainly. I looked over at Lieutenant Dwyer, who seemed to be just as stricken as the rest of them. She shook her head at me and bent over a thick stack of paperwork at her desk.

The ward was completely full, and it seemed strange that none of them were down at physical therapy. I looked at Jack, who was in bed, curled up on his side, with his face turned away from me. Then I looked across the aisle at Vincent, who — wasn't there.

I might have gasped, but I hope I didn't. Quickly, I looked up and down the entire ward, and found only one empty bed.

Vincent's.

Now Lieutenant Dwyer got up and motioned me out to the hallway. I followed her, and she closed the door behind us.

"What happened to him?" I asked, even though I already knew. Except for the details.

"It was an embolism," she said, and blinked a few times. "It just happened a little while ago. I mean, sometimes — especially with paraplegic patients, we —" She stopped. "I don't think it was *three minutes* before I got a doctor up here, but —" She stopped again. "You can't predict an embolism. Sometimes, they just happen."

I saw him a week ago, and he had been *fine*. But everyone in that ward had seen him maybe an *hour* ago, and he had been fine then, too. "Should I —" I had no idea what to say. "Do you want me to —"

"Next week," she said. "Okay?"

I nodded, almost surprised that I still remembered how to do that. "I'm sorry," I said. "Tell them I'm sorry, okay?"

"I will," Lieutenant Dwyer said, and went back into the ward.

Vincent had survived fighting in a war, he had survived becoming paralyzed — and he had died because of a tiny, freak accident inside one of his veins.

But if you ask me, *Vietnam* is what killed him.

I *hate* Vietnam.

April 12, 1968

It's Good Friday, and I know I should be sitting in church, feeling mournful for all sorts of religious 157 reasons.

But, instead, I'm sitting in my room, feeling miserable because a really nice guy I was just getting to know died this week.

What an absolute and total *waste*.

April 15, 1968

I wasn't sure if I wanted to go back to the VA — I mean, I could just *quit,* and what could they do about it? Nothing. I was only a volunteer. I could go away *forever,* if I wanted.

But, I went back.

The ward was quiet, but not in the same stunned, devastated way it was a week ago. A few guys were talking, some were moving around on their crutches or in their wheelchairs, and the room looked almost the way it was before.

It just felt as though all of the life had gone out of it. Mainly because — I could tell the second I looked over at him, lying on his bed — a lot of the life had gone out of Jack.

Instead of waiting for instructions, or advice, from Lieutenant Dwyer, I walked right over there, and sat down in a chair next to him. He glanced up at me, and then looked away.

"I'm really sorry," I said.

Jack nodded.

"So, you want me to leave?" I asked.

He nodded.

"I think I'll stay," I said.

There was a long pause, and then he sighed.

I nodded, and we just sat there together, quietly.

For the rest of the afternoon.

April 16, 1968

I felt funny about going, but today was Opening Day at Fenway Park, and my father bought tickets for us months ago. So, we went, along with my Uncle Colin and my cousin Phil. I wasn't about to bring it up, but I don't think I've ever been to a Red Sox game without Patrick before. So, this just wasn't the same.

But then again, what *was* the same, anymore? Nothing, as far as I could tell.

Actually, one thing was the same: the Red Sox. Even though they won the pennant last year, today they seemed to be back to their old, underachieving selves. They played the Detroit Tigers, and they lost 9 to 2.

Since our star pitcher, Jim Lonborg, is injured — he tore up his knee skiing last winter — we don't have very high hopes for the team this season. And Tony Conigliaro, who got beaned last season, still hasn't recovered the vision in his eye, and so even though he's really young, he's probably going to have to retire. But we have Carl Yastrzemski, and how many teams would like to be able to say *that*?

They're still the Red Sox, and we love them, win or lose. Sometimes I think we love them *more* when they lose.

Lucky for us.

April 19, 1968

I don't want to write this. I don't want to *think* about this. My parents and I were just finishing breakfast this morning, when the doorbell rang. My father opened the door, and it was a man from Western Union, delivering an urgent telegram from the United States Marine Corps. Patrick is in the hospital in some place called Quang Tri, and the telegram said that he was in "extremely grave" condition. That means they don't think he's going to survive.

Oh, my God.

April 21, 1968

My father has been calling everyone from our state representative, to the Red Cross, and all the way up to the Pentagon, trying to get more information about how Patrick is, and *where* he is. But no one seems to know. A lot of our relatives have been coming by ever since we found out, and Brenda and the kids have spent the night here for the last couple of days. My grandmother has been sleeping here, too.

I think my father was just about ready to go out to the airport and try to buy a ticket to Vietnam, when we got another telegram. This one said that Patrick had been upgraded from "grave condition" to "critical condition," and that he's still at the surgical hospital in Quang Tri. It said that he was wounded during a rocket attack, but other than the phrase "suffered multiple fragmentation wounds," we have no idea what sort of injuries he has.

I don't think my mother has eaten or slept since Friday, and she looks just awful. I guess we all do.

Why won't they let us know what's going on?

April 22, 1968

I called Lieutenant Dwyer at the VA to let her know why I wouldn't be coming in today, and to see if she had any idea how we could find out what was really going on with my brother. She offered to make a few calls herself, and see if she could get anywhere — and I definitely didn't try to stop her.

In the meantime, we got another telegram that said that Patrick's condition had now been upgraded to "serious," and they were optimistic that he might be able to recover.

Lieutenant Dwyer called back to tell me she hadn't been able to find out anything more than what little we already knew, and that she was very sorry, and hoped that Patrick would be okay. I thanked her several times, since I really appreciated her trying to help us. I guess we're just stuck doing what we've been doing from the moment he left the country.

Waiting.

April 24, 1968

Patrick called! And I missed it, because I was at school. Dad missed it, too, because he was at the firehouse. But, Patrick called! Mom says it was a terrible connection, and he didn't talk very long, but that he's in Japan at some military hospital, and he thinks they're going to be flying him back to the States in about ten days. She says he also told her — about twenty times — that he's okay, and for us not to worry about him. He promised that he would try to call again, and that he couldn't wait to see us.

He couldn't wait?

April 29, 1968

Since there isn't much I can do sitting around the house after I get home from school, I went over to the VA this afternoon. When I walked in, I could tell that the whole ward had heard about what had happened, because they all started asking me questions right away. We haven't had any more updates since Patrick called last week, but I told them that he was in Japan, and all we knew was that he'd gotten hurt in some kind of rocket attack.

At least ten of the guys insisted that if the hospital staff in Japan had let him talk on the phone, then he had to be in pretty good shape. Otherwise, they would have had someone call for him. I decided to believe them, since after all, they'd all been through it themselves, and knew how it worked.

And I also noticed that despite all of the problems they were facing, they were knocking themselves out to try and cheer *me* up.

They're all really great guys. As far as I'm concerned, anyone who says bad things about Vietnam veterans . . . just doesn't know any.

May 6, 1968

Patrick is supposed to be arriving at the Philadelphia Naval Hospital either late tonight or early tomorrow morning. My parents decided that we should start driving down there today, so that we can see him as soon as possible. It's just going to be the three of us on this trip, and Brenda and Hank will drive down next weekend.

It was about an eight-hour drive, and I fell asleep near Bridgeport and didn't wake up until we were in

New Jersey. That meant that I had completely missed New York — a place I've always wanted to see — but I had a feeling I was going to get plenty of chances.

I think we're going to be making this drive *a lot* during the next few months.

My father had made reservations at a Howard Johnson's motel, just outside Philadelphia. By the time we got there, it was too late to go over to the hospital. So, we just checked in, and then had a quick supper at the restaurant. I don't even remember what I ate, except that I was so hungry that I finished all of it.

I can't wait until tomorrow.

May 7, 1968

We saw Patrick today. Finally!

The minute we walked into his ward, my mother burst into tears and, I cried, too. Patrick was propped up in his hospital bed, looking thin and exhausted, and covered with bandages. He had probably lost about forty pounds, which made his cheekbones seem sharp and his eyes look much darker than usual. Sunken, almost. I could see a chest tube running out of the left side of his chest, his left arm and shoulder were bundled up inside an extra-large sling, and his left leg looked as though it was in *really* bad shape, with small red stains seeping through the layers of bandages.

But, when he saw us, he grinned, and gave a little wave with his right hand.

My father's eyes were bright, and he was saying, "Welcome home, son," while my mother cried and tried to hug him, without touching any of the bandages. That was pretty much impossible, so she clutched his right hand, instead. I think Patrick wanted to cry, too, because he kept swallowing and blinking his eyes a lot.

We spent the whole day there, except when doctors and nurses came by to examine him, or give him medication, and asked us to step outside for a minute. My mother cornered one of the doctors, who told her that they were a little concerned about how well Patrick's leg was going to heal, but otherwise, he was a big tough kid, and that there was no reason for them to think that he wouldn't make a full recovery.

Which made my mother start crying all over again.

We stayed until visiting hours were over. Half of the time we all talked at once, and the rest of the time, no one had much to say. But we really didn't *need* to say anything. All that mattered was that Patrick was here, and we were all together.

When the night-duty nurse finally asked us to leave, obviously we didn't want to go, but my mother promised him that we'd be back, first thing in the morning. There was some more awkward, one-sided hugging, and hand squeezing, and some more crying, too.

Once my parents and I were out in the hall, I suddenly knew that I needed to go back for a minute. So I told them I'd forgotten something, and I'd meet them at the car. Then I slipped into the ward, trying to avoid the duty nurse.

Patrick had sunk back onto his pillow, and I could see tears running down his cheeks. When he saw me, he quickly rubbed the sleeve of his good arm across his eyes.

"I'm not sure I told you I love you," I said. "Or how much I missed you, or how *glad* I am that you're back."

He tried to smile at me, but there were still tears in his eyes. "I didn't want to tell Mom and Dad, but — they're not sure they're going to be able to save my leg."

One thing I had learned at the VA was how *not* to

flinch. "Whatever happens, it'll be okay," I said. "I promise."

"I hope so," he said in a whisper.

I bent down to kiss him on the forehead and then straightened up. "See you in the morning, okay?"

"Yeah." Then he smiled at me shakily. "Still think I'm a big jerk for signing up?"

I knew a test when I heard one. "Yeah," I said. "And a cretin and a moron and an idiot and a dolt. But — welcome home, anyway."

I wasn't sure if he was going to laugh, but then he did, and I did, too.

"At least I'm a *patriotic* cretin, right?" he said.

I nodded, and we held hands tightly for a few seconds. "A *very* patriotic cretin," I said, and we grinned at each other.

My brother was home. He was alive. He was *safe*.

Thank God.

Epilogue

Exactly four weeks later, on June 5, 1968, Senator Robert Kennedy was assassinated, just moments after winning the California primary.

Patrick spent the next eight months in the Philadelphia Naval Hospital, recuperating from his injuries, and fortunately, the doctors were able to save his left leg. Molly and her parents visited him as often as possible, and were very relieved when he finally came home to Boston. For the next few months, Patrick continued to have a difficult time recovering from his wounds — and the war. Molly devoted as much time as possible to helping her brother get better. When she finally woke up one morning because she heard a *thump* coming from his bedroom, as he started doing his daily push-ups again, she knew that he was going to be okay.

In the fall of 1969, Molly started her freshman year at Radcliffe, where she had received a full academic scholarship. She had planned to prepare for her veterinary career, but she soon realized that history and political science interested her even more.

After graduating from Radcliffe, she attended law school at Yale University. By then, Patrick was a member of the Boston Fire Department, and he had married Audrey Taylor. Molly's father was getting ready to retire from the department after thirty years of service, and much to her delight, her mother began taking night courses at Boston University, studying English literature. And Brenda was staying very busy raising four children, after the birth of her twins, Michael and David, in 1971.

Once she graduated from law school, Molly decided to take the bar exam in Massachusetts, as well as New York State. After she passed both of them with flying colors, she moved to New York City, where she got a job with the public defender's office. Although she found the work challenging, it was also often frustrating. She did receive one nice benefit from her time with the public defender's office. After one particularly long and drawn-out case had been completed, she went out to dinner with the assistant district attorney who had been the prosecutor. His name was Jerry Burke, and he was a Vietnam veteran who had served with the 101st Airborne Division in the Central Highlands. Within weeks, they were dating seriously, and within *months*, they got married.

Jerry still works for the Manhattan District Attorney's office, but Molly now specializes in defending wrongly convicted defendants, and has been successful in helping many innocent citizens regain their freedom.

Molly and her husband live in a brownstone building in Brooklyn, New York. They have three teenage children, two dogs, and four cats.

All six of the animals are former strays.

Life in America
in 1968

Historical Note

In the years following the Allied victory in World War II, the United States moved into a period of prosperity, confidence, and great optimism.

The 1950s were a time of innocence and conformity. But there was one dark threat looming — the ever-present possibility of nuclear war with the Soviet Union. Politicians warned constantly about the evils of Communism, which was the form of government practiced by Russia, China, and a number of other countries.

Then, starting in the mid-fifties, a major societal change took place. The civil rights movement began, as African American citizens rebelled against years of segregation and "Jim Crow" laws, that subjected them to constant, oppressive discrimination. During the next few years, segregation lines were broken in schools, restaurants, and many other formerly restricted areas. As reality sank in, the image of a perfect America had begun to shatter.

In 1960, John F. Kennedy was elected President, and

the country was filled with hope. But the threat of Communism still lurked, as the United States clashed with the Soviet Union and Cuba, during famous confrontations like the Bay of Pigs disaster and the Cuban Missile Crisis. The United States also became increasingly involved with political struggles in Vietnam. Even so, there was a great feeling of optimism throughout the United States.

All of that changed on November 22, 1963, when President Kennedy was assassinated in Dallas, Texas. Every American who was alive that day, and old enough to know what was going on, will always remember exactly where he or she was and what they were doing when they heard the news. To make the nightmare even worse, the suspect, Lee Harvey Oswald, was then murdered on national television by a man named Jack Ruby. This only added to the horror all of America felt. All too soon, real-life violence would start appearing regularly on television, but in 1963, it was completely shocking and unprecedented.

Vice President Lyndon B. Johnson took over as President, vowing to continue the policies begun by President Kennedy. While President Johnson was successful in his wide-ranging domestic legislation, most of his achievements have been overshadowed by his support of the Vietnam War.

The United States had been sending military aid and advisors to Vietnam for many years. The goal was to help South Vietnam achieve democracy, and to defend itself from the Communist guerrilla forces of North Vietnam. America feared the possibility of "a domino effect." In other words, their theory was that if Vietnam became a completely Communist country, soon other nations in the area — including Laos, Cambodia, and Thailand — would also fall to Communism.

In August 1964, an American ship was threatened in the Gulf of Tonkin near North Vietnam. Congress passed emergency legislation, which permitted President Johnson to use military force. The President authorized bombing raids over North Vietnam, and by 1965, the first Marines were landing in Danang, South Vietnam. President Johnson had promised that he would never send "American boys" to Southeast Asia to fight a war that the South Vietnamese should fight themselves. Now that this promise had been broken, many Americans felt betrayed and antiwar protests began taking place on college campuses and in large cities.

As the war intensified, there were not nearly enough

volunteers to fill the constant demands for fresh troops. So the Selective Service Board sent out draft notices to thousands of young American men every month. There were only a few ways to get a deferment and avoid serving in the military. Attending college gave young men "student deferments," as long as they maintained passing grades. It became popular for students to burn their draft cards during antiwar demonstrations, although considering the fact that they already had deferments, this really did not accomplish very much. It just looked good on television. Another way to avoid the draft was to obtain a medical deferment for conditions such as being grossly overweight or underweight, having flat feet, or having a heart murmur. A young man could also register to be a "conscientious objector," a person who has religious, moral, or ethical barriers to fighting. Others actually left the country and went to Canada or Europe or to some other place beyond the reach of the American government.

However, hundreds of thousands of other young men answered their draft notices and agreed to serve their country. It is not well publicized to this day, but there were also many more volunteers than most people realize. Young men and women who volunteered tended to be very patriotic, and usually had a strong tradition of military service in their families.

Even today, Americans fiercely debate whether it was right for people to avoid the draft — and also, whether or not it was right to serve in Vietnam. But at the time, these were complicated, difficult decisions, and *no one* was sure what the right answers were. The country was sharply divided on both sides of the issue back in the 1960s — and many people still grapple with it today.

The year 1968 is considered by most historians to be the turning point of the war. On January 21, the Marines at Khe Sanh came under siege, and for the next seventy-seven days, the entire country was riveted by the struggles of those young men out in the lonely red clay hills of Vietnam. At the end of January, the North Vietnamese Army and the Viet Cong mounted a massive countrywide attack known as the Tet Offensive. At one point, enemy soldiers even occupied the American Embassy in Saigon. Although the NVA and VC were ultimately defeated in these attacks, Americans did not like what they were seeing on television and reading in the newspapers. More and more people began to turn against the war.

In late March of that year, President Johnson stunned

the country by announcing that he would not run for reelection. At that point, Senator Robert Kennedy (brother of President John F. Kennedy) became the overwhelming favorite to win the Democratic nomination, instead of his opponent, Senator Eugene McCarthy. Both men were running on antiwar platforms, but Senator Kennedy also spent a great deal of his time making speeches about bringing Americans back together and trying to overcome the turbulence and anger of the times.

Without a doubt, Americans *were* at war with one another during the 1960s. Too often, peaceful demonstrations turned violent, as Americans who held opposing views about the war confronted one another. There were two particularly famous incidents of this nature. During the 1968 Democratic Party Convention in Chicago, antiwar protestors clashed with police officers and National Guardsmen. Hundreds of people were arrested — and hundreds more were injured. Then, during a demonstration at Kent State University in 1970, National Guardsman opened fire on a group of protestors, killing four young students.

Although the Vietnam War was the main focus of most protests, American faced many other challenges during the 1960s. Dr. Martin Luther King, Jr., was the most famous leader of the civil rights movement, and he preached a philosophy of peaceful, nonviolent protest. But racist attitudes were strongly entrenched in many parts of the country, so social changes took place very slowly. Many members of the black community became impatient, and some formed more radical groups, such as the Black Panthers, who had a more violent, "by any means necessary" outlook. After hundreds of years of discrimination, frustrations within the black community had reached the boiling point.

After Dr. Martin Luther King was assassinated in April 1968, there were riots in at least one hundred and twenty-five cities across the country for the next week.

Then, two months later, in June, Senator Kennedy was also assassinated, moments after winning the California Presidential primary. Violence was now becoming a daily part of American life, and it is safe to say that the events of 1968 stunned the entire country. In November, Republican Richard M. Nixon was elected President, after promising to end the Vietnam War. His slogan was "Peace with Honor," although he never really accomplished it.

Vietnam and civil rights were not the only issues dividing Americans. Women began actively campaigning for equal rights and led many protests of their own. The gay rights movement also began during the 1960s. In addition, young people all over the country were actively rebelling against all forms of authority. Although they actually preferred the term "the Beautiful People," these young protesters became popularly known as "hippies." Hippies traditionally had long hair, wore psychedelic clothes, and openly embraced concepts like "sex, drugs, and rock & roll." The Woodstock Festival of Music and Art Aquarian Exposition in August 1969 is probably the most famous hippie event, as thousands of young men and women gathered in rural New York for three days of peace, love, and music.

As the 1960s turned into the 1970s, the Vietnam War began winding down as President Nixon ordered regular troop withdrawals. There was no clear-cut victory: America simply left Vietnam. An official cease-fire was signed in 1973, and on paper, the Vietnam War was over. Nevertheless, the North Vietnamese continued to fight in South Vietnam, and in 1975, they took over the entire country. Now the war *was* over — and democracy was not the winner.

The cultural fallout from the 1960s continues to reverberate today. While American society has not yet achieved universal equality, the country has made remarkable progress in that area in a very short period of time — particularly when compared to many other countries around the world. It seems inevitable that this progress will continue, and that one day, all Americans — regardless of race, creed, religion, or gender — really *will* be treated with complete equality and respect. The United States is also much more cautious about entering into military situations now, and this more thoughtful outlook may help lead the way to world peace in the years to come. Ideally, American will learn from both its successes — and its failures — in the past, and continue moving forward to a positive and hopeful future.

College students gather at Boston Common to show support for the U.S. military presence in Vietnam and to oppose antiwar demonstrators.

A large crowd assembles in front of the State House in Boston to protest the U.S. involvement in the Vietnam War.

At a rally in Boston, young men burn their draft cards in protest of the Vietnam War.

"Beautiful people," more commonly known as hippies, congregate in 1969 on Max Yasgur's dairy farm at the Woodstock Festival of Music and Art Aquarian Exposition, which took place in upstate New York. Billed as "Three Days of Peace and Music," the festival proved to be the culmination of the cultural revolution of the '60s.

Americans went into a state of shock following the November 1963 assassination of President John F. Kennedy by Lee Harvey Oswald. J.F.K., as he was affectionately called, was elected the 35th president of the United States at the age of forty-three. His youthfulness and energy filled the American people with idealism and hope for a better society.

Senator Robert "Bobby" Kennedy, the younger brother of J.F.K., was campaigning for the 1968 presidential election in Los Angeles, California, when a man named Sirhan Sirhan assassinated him. Many voters had believed that Bobby Kennedy, who was often compared to his older brother, would save the country from sinking deeper into the war in Vietnam.

Reverend Martin Luther King, Jr., locks arms and holds hands with fellow activists as they march down Constitution Avenue in Washington, D.C., in 1963 to protest the absence of civil rights for African Americans.

The Feminine Mystique, *by Betty Friedan, was published in 1963 and has sold more than one million copies. The book is credited with launching the Second Wave of the feminist movement, as it changed the consciousness of the country with its insights into a woman's role in society. Friedan defined the "feminine mystique" as the state of mind of women who were confined to their homes and domestic roles without hope of anything more. Friedan founded N.O.W. (National Organization of Women) in 1966.*

In May 1970, students of Kent State University in Ohio organized a demonstration protesting the Vietnam War. When the National Guard was called in to disperse the crowd, the gathering turned violent. Tear gas was fired, and the soldiers opened fire on the students. When the smoke and gas cleared, four students were discovered dead.

A veteran of the Vietnam War visits the Vietnam Veterans Memorial, erected in 1982, in Washington, D.C.

Acknowledgments

☮

Grateful acknowledgment is made for permission to reprint the following:

Cover Portrait: Karen Petrie Medsger, photo courtesy Laurie Petrie Roche.

Cover Background: Jeff Albertson, Stock, Boston.

Page 183 (top): Pro-war demonstration, AP/Wide World Photos.

Page 183 (bottom): Antiwar protest, Ellis Herwig/Stock, Boston.

Page 184 (top): Draft card-burning, Bettmann/CORBIS.

Page 184 (bottom): Woodstock, Bill Eppridge/Timepix.

Page 185 (top): J.F.K.'s assassination, Carl Mydans/Timepix.

Page 185 (bottom): Robert F. Kennedy, UPI/CORBIS.

Page 186 (top): Civil Rights March, UPI/CORBIS.

Page 186 (bottom): *The Feminine Mystique,* by Betty Friedan, Dell Publishing, New York, NY, 1964.

Page 187 (top): Kent State University, Reuters NewMedia Inc./CORBIS.

Page 187 (bottom): Vietnam veteran, AP/Wide World Photos.

Look for My Name Is America:

The Journal of
Patrick Seamus Flaherty

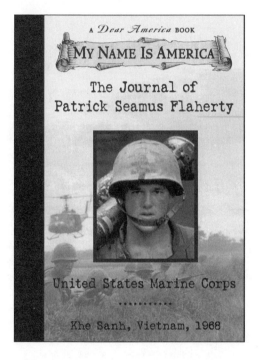

A *Dear America* BOOK

MY NAME IS AMERICA

The Journal of
Patrick Seamus Flaherty

United States Marine Corps

• • • • • • • • • • •

Khe Sanh, Vietnam, 1968

Read this harrowing companion journal of Molly's brother,
an American Marine fighting in Vietnam. Scared but
brave, Patrick must deal with all of the dangers and
emotions of daily life in a war zone.

In honor of all the members of the fire service,
particularly the heroes of the FDNY.

Copyright © 2002 by Ellen Emerson White.

All rights reserved. Published by Scholastic Inc.
557 Broadway, New York, New York 10012.
DEAR AMERICA®, SCHOLASTIC, and associated logos are trademarks
and/or registered trademarks of Scholastic Inc.

Library of Congress Cataloging-in-Publication Data
White, Ellen Emerson.
Where have all the flowers gone? : the diary of Molly MacKenzie Flaherty /
by Ellen Emerson White.
p. cm. — (Dear America)
Summary: In 1968 Massachusetts, after her brother Patrick goes to fight in Vietnam, fifteen-
year-old Molly records in her diary how she misses her brother, volunteers at a
Veterans' Administration Hospital, and tries to make sense of the Vietnam War and
tumultuous events in the United States. Includes historical notes.
ISBN 0-439-14889-8
[1. Vietnamese Conflict, 1961–1975 — United States — Juvenile fiction.   2. Vietnamese
Conflict, 1961–1975 — United States — Fiction.   3. Nineteen sixties — Fiction.
4. Brothers and sisters — Fiction.   5. Diaries — Fiction.   6. United States — History —
1961–1969 — Juvenile Fiction.   6. United States — History — 1961–1969 — Fiction.
7. Boston (Mass.) — Fiction.]   I. Title.   II. Series.
PZ7+
[Fic] — 21   00-020200

10   9   8   7   6   5   4   3   2   1   02   03   04   05   06

The display type was set in Bradley Hand ITC. The text type was set in Bembo.
Book design by Elizabeth B. Parisi
Photo research by Dwayne Howard and Zoe Moffitt

Printed in the U.S.A. 23
First printing, June 2002